I0452879

THE TWIN MYSTERY

THE TWIN MYSTERY
OR, A DASHING RESCUE

NICHOLAS CARTER

WILDSIDE PRESS

Copyright © 2021 by Wildside Press LLC.
Introduction copyright © 2021 by John Betancourt.
Originally published March 21, 1905, by Street & Smith.
Published by Wildside Press LLC.
wildsidepress.com | bcmystery.com

INTRODUCTION

Nick Carter is a fictional character that began as a dime novel private detective in 1886 and has appeared in a variety of formats over more than a century. He first appeared in the story paper *New York Weekly* (Vol. 41 No. 46, September 18, 1886) in a 13-week serial, *The Old Detective's Pupil; or, The Mysterious Crime of Madison Square*.

The character was conceived by Ormond G. Smith, the son of one of the founders of Street & Smith, and realized by John R. Coryell. The character proved popular enough to headline its own magazine, *Nick Carter Weekly*. The serialized stories in *Nick Carter Weekly* were also reprinted as stand-alone titles under the New Magnet Library imprint.

By 1915, *Nick Carter Weekly* had ceased publication and Street & Smith had replaced it with *Detective Story Magazine*, which focused on a more varied cast of characters. There was a brief attempt at reviving Carter in 1924–27 in *Detective Story Magazine*, but it was not successful.

In the 1930s, due to the success of *The Shadow* and *Doc Savage*, Street & Smith revived Nick Carter in a pulp magazine (called *Nick Carter Detective Magazine*) that ran from 1933 to 1936. Since the Doc Savage character had basically been given Nick's background, Nick Carter was now recast as a hardboiled detective. Novels featuring Carter continued to appear through the 1950s, by which time there was also a popular radio show, *Nick Carter, Master Detective*, which aired on the Mutual Broadcasting System network from 1943 to 1955.

The Twin Mystery is taken from Magnet Library #304, dated September 2, 1903.

—John Betancourt
Cabin John, Maryland

CHAPTER I.

THE BROWN ROBIN.

"Mr. Nick Carter:

"I have come to town to do business. I give you notice before I begin, because I am quite certain you will be informed immediately after I commence operations. It really makes little difference; you cannot reach me. Really, my dear Nick, I have a contempt for the so-called detective ability. You, with your Ida, Chick, and Patsy, are a little better than the rest, but you are in the same running when you undertake to stop me.

"The Brown Robin."

This letter Nick Carter found in his mail one morning a short time ago, on coming to his breakfast table.

He read the letter with some interest, noting that it had been mailed late the afternoon before, and in the sub-district in which he lived.

Tossing it over to his wife, Edith, to read, he said:

"That might be taken for a challenge, I suppose."

Edith read it, and replied that she should take it for an impertinence.

"Who is the Brown Robin?" she asked.

"Ah! That is the great mystery," answered Nick.

"A woman?" asked Edith.

"When you ask that question in that way," replied Nick, "you mean to make the statement that you believe it to be a woman."

"Well, yes; I judge the writer of this is a woman."

"Why?"

"The writing, in the first place."

"That will hardly do. It might be taken for the writing of a woman a little more masculine than is usual, or of a man a little more feminine than is usual. I carefully examined the writing before I gave you the letter, and could not determine satisfactorily to myself which it was."

Edith again examined the letter, and said that she should be afraid, after a second look, to stand on either side.

"The truth is, Edith," said Nick, "it is an assumed hand, not the natural one of the person who wrote it, and is not always employed by that person. That is my belief."

Again Edith studied the letter.

"There is something about the whole thing," she said, "that impresses me with the notion that the writer of this is a woman. But if you were to ask me why, I could not tell you."

Nick laughed.

"It is the same old story of puzzling mystery."

"Then you know something of the Brown Robin?"

"I know that the Brown Robin puzzled and mystified the police of Chicago two winters ago. I was appealed to then to go to Chicago, take up the case, and ferret out the mystery, but then I was engaged in an important matter here and could not go.

"Suddenly the Brown Robin disappeared from Chicago and turned up in Boston, where the police were put at their wits' end in an endeavor to detect the person.

"As suddenly he, she or it flitted to Philadelphia, with a like result, and then back again to Chicago. Now it would seem that the Brown Robin is making New York its roosting place."

"But who is the Brown Robin, and what does it do?"

"As I said, who the Brown Robin is—whether a he, she, or it—is a mystery. What the Brown Robin does is to extort money from various kinds of people, and most successfully, by blackmail.

"The Brown Robin moves about so skillfully and shows up in so many guises, that he, she or it has always escaped detection, and has left the police of each place where it has operated in doubt whether it is a man, or a woman, or a lot of men and women, moving under the directions of a very skillful person.

"That is all I can tell you, for I have not looked deeply into the matter."

"This is a direct challenge to you."

"Yes, but I shall not accept it, unless I am retained by a victim of the Brown Robin's arts, and then only if the victim will consent to be guided wholly by me in the matter."

He tossed the letter aside and finished his breakfast. He had hardly time to open his morning paper, when the servant entered with a note, which, she said, had been brought by a messenger boy.

Opening it, Nick read:

"My Dear Carter:
    "Very shortly after receiving this you will have a call from Mr. Alpheus Cary. He is my first victim in New York. I should judge by

this experience that New York is very easy to work. The incident afforded me a good deal of amusement, for Mr. Alpheus Cary hates to give up.

"He was in a panic when he did, but regretted it a minute after. Indeed, my operation came perilously near robbery, for his hesitancy began before he really handed the money over.

"The only regret I have is that the sum was so small. In that sense it was not a brilliant beginning in New York. But you can complete the operation by getting a stiff retainer out of him. Then, if you choose to "whack up," why, you can send me half. That proposition is the reason why I write.

"Really, Carter, there is quite a stroke of business to be done by us in this way. I know you pose as an honest man, but, pshaw! let there be no nonsense between us.

"The Brown Robin."

The first sensation Nick experienced on reading this letter was that of anger. Then the audacity of the writer excited his sense of humor.

"You thought the other letter was impertinent," said he, handing the last one to Edith, "but what do you think of this one?"

Edith read it with flushed face, but, inspired by an idea, she said:

"Nick, if I were you I would capture that person, no matter what I did to accomplish it."

"What would you do?"

"I'd pretend to enter into a bargain with the Brown Robin, such as is here proposed."

Nick did not reply at once. When he did, he said:

"Do you know, Edith, I am under the impression that this is an impudent and audacious beginning of an effort to blackmail me."

"Nick Carter!"

"Yes, a trap is being laid for me to walk into, of which this is only one of the strings."

"But why should they attempt to blackmail you?"

"I suppose my money is as good to them as that of any other person. But what a triumph it would be to have the boast that Nick Carter had been trapped that way!"

"True."

"Edith, let me warn you to be prepared for any trick. Whether I will or not, the Brown Robin has thrown down the gauntlet."

"Do you know Mr. Alpheus Cary?"

"I only know that there is a person of that name, who is a man of wealth and the president of a bank in this city—a man of some prominence, but that is all I do know of him."

"Where does he live?"

"Somewhere in Central Park West, but just where I don't know. What are you thinking of?"

"I was thinking that perhaps the Cary whom you are told will call on you might be the Brown Robin made up, and that it would be well to send Chick or Patsy to find if he is at home."

"Good, Edith," cried Nick, with a laugh, "you are getting to be a great detective. Well, I shall act on your suggestion, only I shall send Ida to Mr. Cary's house, for she is near by."

He went to the 'phone and rang up Ida, and received an immediate response. But Edith, closely watching, saw him start as a look of deep suspicion came over his face.

He made a quick signal to his wife. Asking through the 'phone whether he was talking to Ida, he received an answer which brought again the suspicious look to his face. But he continued, as usual, though his message was a surprise to Edith. He said:

"As soon as you can, Ida, I want you to go to Herman Hartwig, and, giving him the word 'Passen,' tell him to give you his report. Then bring it to me. Do you understand?"

Waiting for a response, he said:

"Then repeat what I have said."

He listened, and, as he did, a broad smile came over his face. He hung up the 'phone and rang off, turning to his wife with a queer light in his eyes.

"Why, Nick," asked Edith, "who is Herman Hartwig?"

"I don't know."

"And what is the word 'Passen?'"

"Never heard of it before."

"Then what is the meaning of your message?"

"Nothing. It was diamond cut diamond. That was not Ida on the other end of the line."

"Who, then?"

"I don't know. Perhaps the Brown Robin. The wires have been tampered with in some way. It was not Ida for, if it had been, she would have wanted to know where Herman Hartwig was to be found, since she had never heard of him before, because I invented the name at the moment."

"Then your suspicions were excited at once?"

"Yes; it was a good imitation of Ida's voice, but a certain trick of Ida's speech was wanting, and I was watching for it."

Nick thought a moment; then, hastily stepping to the 'phone, he cut the connecting wires.

"It is the safest way," he said. "Now, Edith, hurry to the drug store on the corner and send for Chick, Patsy and Ida."

As Edith went out, Nick sat down to his paper again, but he had read a short time only when the servant entered with a card, saying that a caller was in the parlor.

He read the card. The name on it was Mr. Alpheus Cary.

Bidding the servant to tell the gentleman that Mr. Carter was engaged for the present, but would see him presently, he continued to read his paper.

His intention was not to see his caller until his aids should arrive, for he meant that Chick should be present at the interview, and Patsy should shadow the caller when he left.

He was thus engaged when Edith returned.

She bore in her hand a card and note, and, as she entered the room, she was about to speak, but Nick checked her with a gesture.

She handed Nick the card and note. Reading the card, Nick looked up with surprise and compared it with one he had just received. It was the same exactly.

Tearing open the note, he read:

"Dear Mr. Carter:
"I beg you will call on me at the Zetler Bank, on a matter of importance, at your earliest convenience. I do not call on you for the reason that I fear the call would become known to a person I desire to keep in the dark.
"Respectfully,

"Alpheus Cary."

"Where did you get these?" whispered Nick.

"At the drug store," returned Edith, also in a whisper. "I was about going out when the druggist called me by name. An elderly gentleman, standing near, started and spoke in a low tone to the druggist, asking if I was Nick Carter's wife.

"Being told that I was, he came to me, handing me his card and this note, with the request that I should give it to you.

"He said that he had intended to call, had even driven past the door, but, on second thought, believed it were not best, and had gone to the drug store, where he was known, and had written the note there."

"And you came directly back with it?"

"Directly."

"Where did Mr. Cary go?"

"He got into a cab and drove down Columbus Avenue."

Nick thought a moment, and said, in a whisper:

"This must have occurred about the time my caller handed in the other card."

He sprang to his feet and hurried to the parlor.

But it was empty. The waiting caller had left without a word.

Nick, calling the servant, inquired if she had seen the caller leave, but she had not, nor could she give any information.

Pursuing his inquiries, all that he could learn was that a moment after Mrs. Carter was seen to enter the front door an elderly-appearing man had darted from it and had gone down the street, hastily, to the west.

Satisfied that a spurious Mr. Cary had called on him that morning, and that the genuine Mr. Cary had accosted his wife in the drug store, Nick returned to his room to await the arrival of his assistants, Chick, Patsy and Ida.

CHAPTER II.

THE WAY OF THE ROBIN.

Nick's passage to the Zetler Bank to see the real Mr. Alpheus Cary was in the nature of a procession.

He had been impressed with the idea that the caller who had announced himself as Mr. Alpheus Cary, had, by some means, come to know that the real Mr. Cary was in the neighborhood, and had fled because of that.

His fleeing seemed to Nick to suggest that in some way this person was either the Brown Robin or some one connected with that person.

The audacity of the effort to impersonate Cary in an interview with Nick further suggested that the person had much confidence in his own skill, and was rather conceited about it.

He thought it probable that he would be put under observation in his next attempt to leave the house.

So he directed Chick to go out and post himself so that he could shadow Nick and see whether he was followed. And, having respect for the skill of this Brown Robin, he sent Patsy out charged with the duty of following Chick, and Ida later to follow Patsy.

Thus it was that when, an hour later, he went out into the street, his passage to the Zetler Bank was in the nature of a procession.

Nick's passage, however, was not direct, for he received a signal from Chick that the latter thought a person was on the track of his chief.

Consequently he took a devious route, turning into many strange places, doubling on his track and doing a number of strange things.

All this time he paid not the slightest attention as to whether or not another person was doing these strange things, for he was relying upon Chick to determine whether any one was on his track.

"Gee!" said Patsy, when, in these doubling turns, he came upon Ida, "what is this game we're getting this morning?"

However, Chick had seen a young man about twenty-five or six, who had made his appearance only as Nick had shown on the street, and whose route was the same as that of the chief.

When Nick had taken to his devious ways on hearing a peculiar huckster's cry behind him, which he knew to be from Chick, this young man had taken to the same devious ways.

When Nick started straight for the bank, this young man had followed, and Chick saw him walk to the very door of the Zetler Bank to watch Nick enter.

Summoning Patsy by signal, he sent him on the trail of this young man, while he awaited the appearance of Nick from the bank.

The wait was a long one.

When Nick presented his name, Mr. Cary came forward in such excitement that Nick thought he would betray himself to every one within hearing.

"I am glad to see you, Mr. Carter," he said. "My business is most important, yet I have been warned——"

"I know," said Nick, calmly, "the Brown Robin. You have been told not to dare to talk to me."

"Why," exclaimed Mr. Cary, "how do you know that?"

"I guessed it," said Nick, with a smile. "But take me somewhere where we can talk aloud and unheard."

Mr. Cary led the way into an inner room, closing the door after him.

"Now," said Nick, "there are certain things I know of this case, but I want you to tell me everything, concealing nothing, not even when it tells against yourself. I shall regard it as a confidential communication. Make neither excuses, nor apologies, but tell the plain truth."

"But I have been warned not to talk to you at all."

"By whom?" asked Nick.

"By some one who signs the letter 'The Brown Robin.'"

"Let me see that letter," demanded Nick.

"Well, I don't know that I ought."

"Now, Mr. Cary," said Nick, sternly, "you were blackmailed last night; indeed, it was more nearly like robbery, for the money was taken from your hands while you were hesitating whether you would pay it over or not."

"You know that? How?" asked Mr. Cary.

"Never mind how I know," replied Nick, sternly. "It is my business to know a great many things. But I want to say this: I mean to investigate this matter to the bottom. If you help me by giving me all the information in your possession, so much the better, but whether you do or not I shall find all out. Now choose which you will do."

"Well, I had intended to retain you, but this letter——"

"Let me see it," demanded Nick, in a decided tone.

Mr. Cary yielded, and, taking the letter from his breast pocket, handed it to Nick.

At a glance the famous detective saw that it was the same handwriting, on the same kind of paper, as the two letters he had received in the morning. It read:

"Dear Papa Cary:

"I want to warn you against a very bad man. His name is Nick Carter. You will only get yourself into trouble if you don't take my warning. You are in a good deal of trouble now, for you stand in danger of exposure. Fie! Such a naughty Papa Cary! But you must not talk to Nick Carter. You must not talk to him of our pleasant experiences last night. And, Papa Cary, you must come again, and bring some more of the stuff that makes the mare go. I shall tell you when and where. And you must, or there will be pretty photographs sent to Mamma Cary and the little Carys, and to the bank officials, and so there will if you talk to Nick Carter.

"The Brown Robin."

Nick folded up the letter and placed it in his pocket, saying:

"This letter will be safer with you than with me. Now tell me how you met the woman."

"How do you know——"

"I would rather you would answer my question," interrupted Nick, sternly, "and please waste no time with questions. You met a woman last night. Where? How? When?"

"Well, it was in the Rideau restaurant—that is a——"

"I know—in Fourth Avenue. How came you to be there?"

"Some business took me on the East Side yesterday afternoon, on which I was delayed beyond my own dinner hour. I had heard of this place and thought I would like to visit it. So I went there to dine. It was crowded, few seats being vacant.

"As I passed down the rows of tables I came to one at which was seated a young woman of attractive appearance, dressed like a lady, in brown, on whose hat was a robin.

"The seat opposite her was vacant, and, bowing, I asked if I could occupy it. She consented by saying that she could not prevent me, as it was free to any one to take.

"Seating myself, it was not long before I was in conversation with her."

"I see," said Nick. "Did she know who you were?"

"Why, no."

"Then how did she come to know?"

"That is where I was a fool. I told her."

"On her inquiry?"

"No, confound it. A bottle of wine and a pretty woman let loose my tongue, and I babbled like an infant."

Nick had difficulty in keeping a straight face over this frank confession and the disgusted face that accompanied it.

"Of course you didn't know her?" asked Nick.

"No; she told me she was but recently from Chicago; that she was married; that her husband had been detained at the last moment, but would soon follow her."

"Well, what then?"

"It ended in my paying for her supper, and we arose from the table together, leaving the restaurant together.

"In the street I asked her direction, and proposed to accompany her as far as her door."

"It would seem as if, then, you took the lead in this thing."

"That is true in a way, yet she encouraged every step."

"Of course. Go on."

"She took me into Seventeenth street, and toward the east, to a respectable-looking house, which she said was one in which she was staying, and asked, indeed coaxed, me to enter.

"Well, like a fool, I consented. She took me into the front parlor, and, asking me to be seated, went off, saying that she would return in a moment."

"She did, having changed her street dress for a flowing wrapper. Seating herself, she began a series of questions about myself that I, fool that I was, answered.

"Suddenly, and without intimation of her purpose, she arose, and, coming to me, threw her arms about my neck, seating herself on my lap.

"I was so astonished at this for a moment I was helpless, and in that moment there was a flash of light that blinded me.

"The woman laughed gayly, and, jumping up, ran into the other room. A moment later she returned, saying:

"'Come, Papa Cary. I don't give my pleasant company for nothing. You've enjoyed my society for two or three hours. You must pay for it. Come! Shell out!'

"'What is this?' I cried, 'blackmail?'

"'Some unpleasant people call it that, I believe,' she said. 'But whatever it is, you must submit.'

"'Not by any means,' I said. 'You have attacked the wrong person.'

"Again she laughed, and, springing up, ran into the next room, to return in a moment, bringing with her a photograph plate.

"'You may look at that,' she said, holding it up before me. Over the rim she pointed a small revolver.

"I looked to see that a photograph of myself, with her on my lap, her arms about my neck, had been taken.

"I fairly staggered back in alarm, and with a merry, mocking laugh, she hurried with the plate into the other room. When she came back, she said:

"'I'm a business woman, Papa Cary. A short horse is soon curried. Out with your money, or, as soon as these photos are printed they will be sent to decorate your home and your office.'

"In my first fright over this threat I took some money from my pocket, but the thought came that payment wouldn't end it, and that I ought to bargain with her in a way that would secure me.

"While I hesitated, thinking what to do, by a quick movement she snatched the money from my hand, crying, with a laugh: 'Thank you.'

"I protested—demanded its return. But she said:

"'Oh, no! You have given me this, and it will not be the last that you will give me, either. This is only the beginning. And I will pay you for it by always keeping those photographs.'

"All this time she was laughing, but I could see in her right hand her revolver. I suddenly jumped forward to seize her revolver arm, when she sprang back and in an instant everything was dark. The lights went out.

"Then I was pushed forward and out of the room by more than one, through a hall and into the street.

"In my anger I threatened that I would put you, Mr. Carter, on her track, and when I was in the street I rushed about, trying to find a policeman.

"By and by, however, my common sense came uppermost, and I saw that by appealing to a policeman I should only make public what I should, in my own interests, keep quiet.

"So, determining to see you as soon as I could, I went home.

"This morning, on reaching the bank, I found the letter which you now have in your possession."

"How much money did she take?"

"A little less than a hundred dollars—I cannot tell exactly; between ninety and a hundred."

"Did you see any one else then?"

"No."

"You could go again to that house?"

"No doubt of it."

"Have you told me everything that occurred?"

"Everything, reserved nothing. Now, I want those photographs, Mr. Carter. I want you to get them. I'll pay for them; but I won't be blackmailed."

Nick was silent a moment or two, thinking. Then he said:

"On your recital it seems to be merely a vulgar panel game. But I think there is more back of it than that. However, I will take the case. I will think it over. Do nothing, however, until you see me again. I shall probably be back again in an hour or two, possibly with my plan of action worked out."

Nick left the banking house, and, going into the street met Chick and Ida.

"Was I followed?"

"Yes," replied Chick. "Followed to these doors by a young fellow of twenty-five, stylishly dressed. He was like a woman more than a man; that is, his face was so fine and handsome."

"What became of him?"

"He went off after seeing you, with a curious smile on his face. Patsy is on his trail."

"Then that is all right," said Nick. "Come with me. I think we have got a case well worth looking on. We will go somewhere where we can talk it over."

The three then went to a neighboring hotel.

CHAPTER III.

A BLIND CHASE.

When Patsy took the trail of the young man who had followed Nick to the doors of the bank, the only purpose of it was to find out who he was and with whom he had connection.

In taking up the trail Patsy was wary. His first effort was to determine whether the young man feared shadowing, and, if he did, whether he believed himself to be shadowed.

For the first ten minutes there were no indications of any kind on the part of the young man.

He took up a bee line for Broadway, and, turning into that thoroughfare, walked to the south with a rapid gait and a businesslike manner, turning neither to the right nor the left, nor giving any heed to persons behind him.

Thus they went, the followed and the follower, down Broadway, when, the building of the New York Life being reached, the young man suddenly turned into it with quickened pace.

Patsy broke into a sharp run. He quickly appreciated the danger he was in of losing his man. It seemed to him that these great big buildings, with their numerous elevators, many stairs and entrances and exits, were especially contrived to favor escaping crooks.

As he dashed through the entrance, he saw his man turning, on a run, into the rotunda, which is circled by elevators.

"The deuce!" cried Patsy. "My one chance is that he can't get an elevator before I get to him."

He ran like a deer down the long corridor, to the amazement of those who were passing.

He turned the corner just in time to see the gates of the elevator close, as it shot upward, and in it was the man he had followed.

This was almost too much for Patsy, and he gave an exclamation of chagrin. But he rapidly took in the fact that the elevator that had just gone up was the one that did not stop short of the tenth floor, and that one was to follow, stopping at each.

Into this he plunged, concealing himself from view, but in such a way that he himself could watch.

Passing the ninth floor, he saw the young man eagerly watching the elevator that followed.

Patsy could not get out on the ninth, but he did on the tenth, and hurried down the stairs. Some one was descending the stairs to the eighth floor. Leaning over the balustrades, Patsy saw a man descending rapidly.

This one wore a dark beard and mustache, and his hair was of the same color. The man he had followed had been beardless and his hair was quite light. But there was something in the carriage of the shoulders of the man descending the steps that suggested the one he had followed down Broadway.

Springing to the head of the stairs, Patsy flung himself on the balustrades, sliding down thence to gain time.

The man followed quickened his pace and fairly flew down the steps two at a time. Patsy was gaining on him, for he was more reckless in his pursuit than the man was in his flight—taking more chances.

Thus the chase continued until the floor on which the great offices of the insurance company were reached, when the followed man plunged into them, with Patsy close on his heels.

Then the man stopped, faced about and waited for Patsy to come up. To the lad's astonishment, he was not in disguise. He looked at Patsy with a sarcastic smile, and asked:

"Are you following me?"

"Yes," replied Patsy, carefully sizing up his man.

"You could be in better business," replied the other. "What are you doing it for?"

"You know very well," replied Patsy.

"Now that you have got up to me, what are you going to do?" he asked.

That was just exactly what Patsy was asking himself. What was he going to do? But he made a bluff, and said:

"I am going to find out who you are, and what your name is."

"That's easy," replied the other. "But what do you want to know for?"

"That's my business," replied Patsy.

The fact was, Patsy didn't really know why he had been ordered to follow the man. He suspected that it was because the man had followed Nick, and that there was a desire to know who he was.

"Of course, that is your business," replied the other. "Very well, my name is George Vernon; I am one of the secret inspectors of this company. I followed Nick Carter this morning, thinking he touched the case I am on, until I found he did not. Then I sheered off. I take it I am a good deal in the same business you are."

All the time he was talking this way he had been edging toward a door.

This seemed to be so straight that Patsy could not deny it, though he believed the fellow was lying. He looked around to the clerks for confirmation, but they were all behind high desks and railings, and he could not get to them except by leaving his man.

A high official of the company approached, one Patsy knew well.

Patsy hailed him, and asked him if the man calling himself Vernon was in the employ of the company.

"Well, that's a hard one for me," said the official, good-naturedly. "I should be greatly puzzled to identify all of our employees."

The man said, respectfully:

"I am in the inspectors' department."

The official, however, became suddenly serious, and asked:

"But what is it? Anything wrong with him, Patsy?"

The other now turned on the lad with a start, his eyes intently fixed on Patsy, and the lad, as much as he respected the high official, could have kicked him for letting out his name.

But the high official did worse. Saying to the one who called himself Vernon to stand where he was, he seized Patsy by the arm to lead him to a gentleman sitting at a desk within a railing.

The impulse was a kindly one, for the high official wanted to serve Patsy, but it was a mistaken one, since the other, seizing his opportunity, dashed through the door, near which he was standing, into a big office beyond.

Patsy broke from the grasp of the high official and jumped after him. There was a second's delay as the door swung back on him, but when he had passed through he saw the other running down the long room.

The sight of a man flying frantically through the room, with another plunging along as frantically, followed closely by a high official of the company, excited all the clerks, and they thronged into the narrow way, so impeding Patsy's pursuit that, by the time he had reached the door at the end of the room through which the other disappeared, his man was nowhere to be seen.

He ran hither and thither toward all the outlets, but quickly recognized the futility of further effort.

He went back to the high official, who had followed him out of the room. Patsy was considerably nettled, but, choking down his anger, said:

"He's a crook, all right, or he wouldn't have wanted to get away from me. But now I want to ask you whether there is a George Vernon in the employ of the company."

"What department does he say he is employed in?" asked the official.

"In the inspector's department."

"Come with me," said the official.

Patsy was led to a room where a man, busily engaged, was seated at a desk. He arose immediately on the approach of the high official, answering promptly the question whether there was a George Vernon in his employ.

"Yes; there is such a person, and he is in the next room at this moment."

"Call him," said the official.

A tall, thin, intelligent-looking young man, the very opposite in appearance of the one whom Patsy had followed, reported.

What was apparent was that the man followed had known of this George Vernon, and had seized on his name to throw Patsy off.

When the real George Vernon was told of the occurrence and of the man who had taken his name, he said that on the day previous he had fallen in with a man of the description given in an uptown hotel, who had expressed a wish to take out a policy on his life. The real Vernon had talked with him on that line and given him his name and department.

"Well," said Patsy, to the high official, "my man got away, but one thing is settled, he's a crook, and the other thing is that I have him so well sized up that I'll know him, I don't care how he is disguised."

Patsy left the offices of the company, and as he did so, he said to himself:

"My man carries his shoulders as not one man in a thousand does. He has a short step and a knock-kneed gait; he has no beard and a small mole under his chin, on the left side."

He stopped in the corridor suddenly, slapped his thigh with his hand, stood still a moment, thinking earnestly. Finally he exclaimed aloud:

"Holy smoke! I'll bet that's the way of it."

Seeking a retired spot, in a corner, he made a rapid change in his appearance.

He had entered the building a smartly dressed young fellow. He left it looking like a broken-down man of sixty, limping in gait and with bowed shoulders, racked with a cough.

But he did not leave it until he had stood some time in the entrance holding out his hands and asking for money of every one that entered nor until he had been fairly driven from it by the officer in charge.

Then he stood on the sidewalk, still begging, and continued to do so until the officer drove him away by threatening him with arrest.

All the while he was thus engaged his eyes had been busy, and he saw a man standing on the opposite side of the street, occupying a position that commanded a view of the main entrance.

When driven from the sidewalk in front of the building he crossed the street and took up a position near this man.

A moment was sufficient to satisfy Patsy that he was disguised. Half an hour passed, during which Patsy begged, when he could without being discovered by policemen, and still shadowed the disguised man, who was watching the main entrance.

Finally this man strolled away like one who did so reluctantly. Patsy watched him with a thrill of delight.

He had found his man again.

The man went to a hotel, where he sat down in the writing-room and, taking paper and envelope from his pocket, began to write letters.

Patsy slipped away and made another change in his appearance, and, coming back, set out to write letters himself.

When the other had written two letters, he got up and went out, followed by Patsy.

This time he went to an American District Telegraph office, handing the letters in and paying the fee.

Leaving the office he went directly back to the hotel where he had written his letters, and, calling for the key of room ninety-eight, said to the clerk:

"I am tired and shall lie down for a nap. Call me by two o'clock. Not later."

He went to his room. Patsy turned over the register and found the name of Harold Stanton, and opposite the number ninety-eight.

"How long has Stanton been staying with you?" asked Patsy.

"Only since last night."

"What do you know of him?"

"Nothing. He paid for his room for two nights. But he wasn't in his room last night."

Patsy went away, saying:

"What next? I've run him down to this place, and know he figures as Harold Stanton."

He went back to the American District Telegraph office and persuaded the man in charge to give him the names of the persons to whom Stanton had written letters.

One was Nick Carter, the other was Alpheus Cary.

Patsy gave a long whistle, and set out to find his chief.

CHAPTER IV.

THE REAL THING.

After Nick had talked over the case with Chick and Ida, he had sent Chick to the house in Seventeenth Street to take stock of it and to make inquiries.

"Chick," he had said, "I don't think you will learn much, for I fancy the house has been abandoned by these people. However, you may learn something in looking it up."

He then went to his house, to find a caller awaiting him. Nick looked at the card, but did not recognize the name. It was Richard F. Mountain.

He sent for the caller to come to his own room.

Mr. Mountain was one who showed in his movements that he was a man of business, and accustomed to affairs.

"Are we alone, Mr. Carter?" he added, on entering. "What I have to say is strictly confidential."

"We cannot be overheard here," replied Nick.

"Then the next question is, can I rely upon you to take my case?"

"I never decide to take a case until I hear the story," said Nick, "but whatever confidence you give me will be respected."

"It's a case of attempted blackmail," replied Mr. Mountain.

"The Brown Robin?" asked Nick.

Mr. Mountain stared a moment before he replied:

"Yes, that name has cropped up in the case."

"Then I take your case," said Nick, "for I am already engaged. Go on with the story."

"I am an insurance agent and real estate broker," said Mr. Mountain, plunging at once into his story, "and frequently have sums of money in my hands for investment belonging to other people. My reputation is good and my standing high.

"Some time ago I was caught in a speculation in which I had ventured rather recklessly. I reached a point where, unless I could put up a very considerable sum, I was likely to lose all I had ventured—lose everything.

"In this strait I used the money of an estate I was managing, and saved myself for that time. It was wrong and was something that people did not believe I would be guilty of.

"After I had passed this money out of my hands an accounting was suddenly and unexpectedly demanded of me. I was in a corner, likely to be exposed and ruined. The facts were not suspected, however, and a day or two intervened. I tried to extricate myself, but could not.

"In my distress I determined on suicide, and drew up a statement which was a confession, placing it in my desk, to be found when my death was announced.

"On the day I had fixed for my death—the day of accounting, I was given a respite by a postponement for one week.

"During that week the speculation I was engaged in was brought to an unexpected and successful conclusion and realization. I was in funds again—in fact, a rich man.

"During the few days left me before the accounting, I was so busy in preparing for it and buying back securities that I had used, that the confession passed from my mind.

"After I had passed through the accounting triumphantly, I looked for it. It was gone. I searched and inquired, but without success.

"For a long time it worried me greatly, but as time went on and nothing came of it, I began to think that I must have destroyed it and forgotten I had done so.

"But yesterday a copy of it was presented to me, and I was told that I could have the copy and the original for fifty thousand dollars.

"I temporized and put off further negotiations until to-morrow. Now, that is the whole story. And, Mr. Carter, I am here to say that I will not pay the sum. I will not be blackmailed. I don't want to be exposed, either; I do not want the disgrace that would follow. My business would be ruined. That is a small matter in one way, for I am a wealthy man, but I do not want to lose the respect and confidence I enjoy.

"In my whole business life I have made this one false step. But, all the same, I will not be blackmailed.

"Now, with handing you this letter, received this morning, I have stated my case."

He took a letter from his pocket and handed it to Nick. At a glance Nick recognized the paper and the handwriting. It read:

"Mr. Richard F. Mountain:

"Contrary to my custom, I gave you two days to comply with my demands. Then I thought you asked for time to gather the money required. Reviewing our talk, I see now that you made no promise. I have been lax. I shall not be again. Tomorrow you must be prepared to comply. I shall call you to a place to pay the money. Be prompt in your coming. But heed this. Do not call in the services of Nick Carter. Do not talk to him at all.

"The Brown Robin."

Holding the letter in his hand, Nick asked:

"How was this demand made?"

"By a young man who called on me at my office yesterday afternoon."

"What name did he give?"

"None. He approached when I was engaged with some people I was doing business with, merely saying:

"This is a copy, but important enough to demand your immediate attention."

"I read it, of course, and, getting up from my seat, took him aside, demanding to know what was wanted.

"His answer was that he was acting for another person, who wanted fifty thousand dollars for the original. Situated as I was, surrounded by people who were at the time placing financial trust in me, I could do nothing but fight for delay and postponement."

"I see," said Nick. "Now, have you any idea who this young man was?"

"No."

"Nor who it is he says he represents?"

"No knowledge."

"Do you suspect any one?"

"Well, I hardly know how to reply. I had a typewriter—a young woman in my employ, who left me suddenly just before I missed that paper. Time and time again my mind has gone back to her in suspicion with nothing to support it. Her name was Alberta Curtis."

"Have you heard of her since she left you?"

"In a way, immediately after her disappearance. She was a Southern girl of a good but impoverished family. She eloped with a married man. That was the cause of her leaving me. I heard of it from her family, who cast her off for the act."

"With whom did she elope?"

"I only know his name—Charles Stymer."

Just then Patsy came in, and Nick sent for him.

"This is Patsy Murphy, Mr. Mountain," said Nick. "One of my most trusted aids. I want to question him on some business he has on hand."

Turning to Patsy, he asked:

"Did you follow your man?"

"Yes. He gave me a chase, too."

"Did you get close to him—close enough to know what he looks like?"

"I had a talk with him."

"Describe him to me?"

Patsy gave an elaborate description of the man that had figured before him both as George Vernon and Harold Stanton.

As Patsy talked, Nick, closely watching Mr. Mountain, saw him show signs of increasing excitement, until he finally burst out:

"Why, he is describing the very man who called on me yesterday."

"Then," said Nick, with a smile, "the Brown Robin is both a man and a woman."

"I do not understand you," said Mr. Mountain.

"Probably not," said Nick. "I am not far enough in the case to understand it myself. We are already engaged on one case of blackmail in which the Brown Robin figures as a woman. Now you give us one in which it figures as a man.

"The Brown Robin has given a good deal of trouble in Chicago, Boston and Philadelphia without being detected.

"It has just begun operations in New York. I imagine your case is the first one of its operations, and the other we have the second.

"Whether it is a he or a she, or a gang, it is bold, audacious and skillful, working in a new way."

"By the way, chief," asked Patsy, "have you received another letter from the Brown Robin?"

"Yes; why do you ask?"

"Because this fellow I followed sent you one."

Nick picked a letter from the table and handed it to Patsy. It read:

"My Dear Uncle:

"Really, you are much better than I supposed. It is worth while working against you. You're not easy, but keep me at work. What a dance you gave me this morning. And your Patsy is a regular laloo. He ran me down and cornered me this morning. If he had dared to arrest me he would have done so, but he had no right to do that, so, of course, he didn't. I slipped away from him only by accident. The above is only by the way. I write to say that you are not serving Papa Cary well. Drop him for his own sake. Even if you do stop him from giving me more, I'll ruin him. That is my rule. His safety is in submitting to me.

"The Brown Robin."

Patsy folded the letter, and handed it back to Nick, saying:

"He wrote another to the other."

"Who?"

Patsy wrote the name of Alpheus Cary on a slip of paper, handing it to Nick.

"Ah! I must know what it said," said Nick, as he glanced at it.

Turning to Mr. Mountain, Nick said:

"One of the peculiar features of this affair is the frequent and impudent letters that are written to me.

"Until you came with your story, I was at a loss to understand the reason of them. I do now. Your case is the big one. While it is being worked the Brown Robin would have us think that the other case is the only one it is working on.

"It is quite ingenious and a new way of working. Leaving a trail open on the second, they will carefully make those to the first blind.

"Now, Mr. Mountain, return to your office. Another aid of mine will call on you as soon as he can. His sole business will be to study your appearance. Give him every opportunity.

"If you receive another letter, let him have it. If you receive a notice from the Brown Robin to go to any particular place, tell him of it. That I must know of at the earliest moment.

"Now, Patsy, Chick is over somewhere in Seventeenth Street. Find him and send him to Mr. Mountain's office. Now get away, please, both of you, for I must go out."

Mr. Mountain returned to his office, feeling a weight off his shoulders, since the celebrated Nick Carter had the case in hand.

Patsy hurried off to find Chick.

Nick himself made his way to the Zetler Bank to find Mr. Cary almost in a state of collapse.

A messenger had brought him a letter from the Brown Robin.

It read:

"Dear Papa Cary:

"Your little present of last night only went a little way. I want more for some expenses I have. You must be at the corner of Fourth Avenue and Twenty-eighth Street this afternoon at five o'clock. Be prompt, now, because there will be some one there to bring you to me. And bring some money. A nice good lot. Don't fail, if you do—
"The Brown Robin."

When Nick had read this letter, Mr. Cary handed him a photograph which he said had been brought in but a short time before, carefully wrapped up.

Nick saw that it was one taken by flashlight. It showed a woman sitting on Mr. Cary's knee, her arms about his neck, his face showing plainly.

Nick thought it was about as compromising a picture as a respectable elderly gentleman of family could be tortured with, and one of which clearly no explanation could be given to offset or contradict the story it told. He studied the woman's face, or so much as she showed. There was art in the way it was shown, yet concealed.

"Tear it up and burn it," he said. "You must not have it lying about your desk."

And while Mr. Cary was engaged in the work of destroying the damaging photograph, Nick was busily thinking.

Finally he asked:

"Have you nerve enough to keep this engagement with the Brown Robin and carry her another hundred dollars?"

Against this Mr. Alpheus Cary protested warmly, declaring that he never again would voluntarily see the woman.

But Nick's persuasive powers must have been great, for shortly after four o'clock Mr. Cary was seen to leave the bank, and had he been followed, it would have been seen that his way was up Fourth Avenue.

CHAPTER V.

THE BROWN ROBIN DINES.

As the hour of five approached, an elderly gentleman who would have been recognized by any of the directors of the Zetler Bank as Mr. Alpheus Cary, its president, could be seen on the corner of Twenty-eighth Street and Fourth Avenue.

He was looking in every direction, and peering into the face of every man who approached him, exhibiting a nervousness and an anxiety which showed that he regarded his mission at that place as everything but pleasant.

Frequently he took out his handkerchief and mopped his face; altogether, he made himself rather conspicuous on the corner.

Finally, as five o'clock was reached, a young man Patsy would have recognized as the one who went to sleep in the hotel after writing two letters, came up from some unknown place, for Mr. Alpheus Cary thought he sprang from the earth.

"Mr. Cary, I believe," said this young man, addressing the elderly gentleman.

"That is my name," replied Mr. Cary, nervously.

"I thought that I recognized you," said the young man.

"Are you the one——"

But he was interrupted.

"How is the market to-day, Mr. Cary?" asked the young man. "My eye has been off the tape to-day, and I am carrying a lot of U. P."

Could any one have been close enough, they would have seen that while the young man was asking this question, and others, and receiving nervous and embarrassed answers to them, he was closely watching the elderly man.

If Mr. Cary had been a sharp detective, he would have thought that these sharp looks meant something, but as he was not, of course, he apparently did not observe them.

Finally the young man said:

"Are you prepared to follow me?"

"Why, yes; that is why I am here, I suppose. Are you the one who was to meet me here?"

"Mr. Cary, are you acting in good faith?"

"Why, yes, what do you mean?"

"Did you come here alone?"

"Entirely so."

"Did any one know of your coming here besides yourself?"

"Not a single person."

"Will you give your word that Nick Carter is not in concealment here to see us go off together and to follow us?"

"I will swear that I am here alone; that neither Nick Carter nor any one else is in concealment here to follow us."

"Very good; I'll take your word for it. But let me tell you that if you have deceived me in any way, that you will be punished in a way that you will not like."

"I have not deceived you. No one is with me, and no one could suspect that I was to be here."

"Come along, then."

The young man led Mr. Cary down Twenty-eighth Street to Lexington Avenue, and, turning the corner, hurried him into a nearby doorway.

"I do not disbelieve you, Mr. Cary, but I am going to be satisfied."

They stood there a while. Evidently satisfied that they were not followed, he motioned for Mr. Cary to follow him.

Their way now was to a rather plain house at the other end of the block.

Reaching it, they mounted the steps, the young man tapping at the door. It was opened immediately, and the young man motioned for Mr. Cary to enter.

Then he followed, closing the door after him.

"Enter the parlor, Mr. Cary," he said, "and I will call the one you came to see."

He disappeared, running up the stairs.

Mr. Cary had a long time to think over the wisdom or unwisdom of his step in again putting himself in the power of the woman who had, the night previous, played him such a scurvy trick.

For one who wanted to see him so badly as she had written, the Brown Robin was slow in making her appearance.

By and by, however, there was a movement on the stairs, in the hall, and Mr. Cary anxiously waiting, heard the Brown Robin's voice saying, rather commandingly:

"You will be here promptly at nine in the morning?"

The voice of the young man who had brought him to the house was heard in reply.

"Yes, my sister; but you will not see me until that time."

The other door opened and closed with a bang.

Mr. Cary grinned on hearing this. But whether in satisfaction of the departure of the young man, or in pleased anticipation of a *tête-à-tête* with the Brown Robin, did not appear.

His face, however, was perfectly composed when the Brown Robin, very cool and elegant in appearance, entered the parlor.

"How good of you, Papa Cary, to come and see me again," she cried. "You may kiss me."

She offered her cheek to Mr. Cary, who hesitated a moment and then, as if he could not resist the temptation, awkwardly kissed her, to her great amusement.

She sat down opposite him, saying:

"I was afraid that you would be angry with me for playing that trick on you."

"Then you mean to give me back that money?" said Mr. Cary.

"Oh, dear no," she cried. "I couldn't do that. You see, I have spent all that money. We had to move this morning, and then my brother, Harold, had some debts that I had to pay. New York is an awfully expensive place, and I want money. You have brought me some, haven't you?"

"I should suppose your husband would supply your needs?" said Mr. Cary. "When does he reach here from Chicago?"

"I hope not soon, Papa Cary, for then I would have to stop seeing you. And I mean to see a good deal of you. Do you know what I am going to do this afternoon? I am going to give you a nice dinner. You gave me a nice one yesterday. Only you'll pay for this one, just as you did for the one yesterday. That is, if you have brought me some money. Have you?"

"Have I?" asked Mr. Cary. "Well, yes, I have brought you some. Here is a hundred dollars."

He handed the roll to her.

"Only a hundred," she said, as she took it. "That is not handsome, Papa Cary. I thought it would be five times as much. But I'll take this, and you will have to give me more money five times as often, if you only give it in such little bits."

"I'll give you a good deal more if you will do something for me I want you to."

"What is that?"

"Give me that photograph plate and the pictures you have had printed."

The Brown Robin laid her shapely head back on the cushions of her chair and laughed long and heartily. Then she said:

"Oh, that poor little trick! You want to bargain with me, Papa Cary. Now, what will you give for them?"

"What would you have the heart to demand?"

"Well, Papa Cary, I have such a soft heart that I am afraid I must let you put the figure on them."

"I will give you a thousand dollars for them."

"Have you the money here?"

"No. I have no more than I gave you. But I would give it on delivery of the plate and pictures."

"And do you think I would give up the pleasure of seeing you for a thousand dollars?"

"That isn't the question."

"Oh, yes it is. Don't you see that it is owing to my having those pictures that you are here to-day? If I hadn't them, you wouldn't be here now, would you?"

"Yes, I think I should, if you had sent for me to come."

The Brown Robin threw her head to one side and eyed the elderly gentleman shrewdly for a while.

"I am afraid you are fibbing, Papa Cary," she said. "And I am getting afraid of you, too. I fear instead of being a respectable, elderly gentleman, ready to give aid and protection to unprotected females, you are a gay old dog.

"No, I can't sell that pretty picture for a thousand dollars. It's too cheap. It cost me too much pains to get it. And then, how do I know but that you will take it to your club, show it around to other gay old dogs, as your last conquest?"

Mr. Cary grinned delightedly over being called a gay old dog, but shook his head and protested with his hands.

"But come," said the Brown Robin, as a servant entered from the rear. "Come to dinner all by our two selves."

She led the way, and Mr. Cary followed into a rear room, where a dinner table was laid.

The dinner was a good one, and Mr. Cary evidently enjoyed it, for he ate heartily, getting quite gay over it.

Of wine, however, he was sparing in use, though urged often to drink.

When the dinner was over Mr. Cary renewed his efforts to get the photographic plate, but the Brown Robin was not to be cajoled into a bargain.

She evaded in every way coming to close quarters, laughing and joking.

Finally she put an end to it all by saying that she must go out, and that Papa Cary could accompany her a part of the way.

She went to the upper part of the house, and while she was gone Mr. Cary seemed to show a most inexcusable curiosity as to the room he was left in and what it contained, for he examined everything in it, picking up a few things which he put in his pocket.

When the Brown Robin returned she was dressed for the street.

"Am I pretty enough to walk with you?" she asked.

"I don't know in which costume you are the prettiest," replied Mr. Cary, "but there is a strange thing," he continued. "I do not yet know your name."

"You shall call me Mrs. Clymer," she said, as she led him out of the door.

She walked with him up Lexington Avenue as far as Thirtieth Street, into which street she turned, going toward Fourth Avenue. She stopped before a certain house and looked at its front carefully.

"Let us go in here," she said.

"What for?"

"To look at it. It is empty. One of those furnished houses to rent. I like to look at them."

Mr. Cary followed her up the stoop. The door was opened by a caretaker who had seen them ascend the steps. Mrs. Clymer, if that was her name, was contented with looking at the parlors.

She went out, and, walking up to Fourth Avenue, turned to the south, Mr. Cary obediently following her.

At Twenty-third Street she turned the corner, going to a real estate office, where she entered into conversation with the broker. Mr. Cary, meantime, looked out of the window into the street.

If he had known them, he would have recognized in the two men standing on the pavement near the door, Chick and Patsy.

But the Brown Robin called him to her, saying:

"I must have twenty-five dollars. I want to pay it to this man."

"I haven't that amount with me," replied Mr. Cary.

"Give me your check, then."

"Oh, I can't do that. But wait a minute. I can get the money."

He hurried out, going quickly to the corner. Here he stopped, sounding a signal. Chick and Patsy, hearing it, went quickly to the corner.

As they came up, Mr. Cary said:

"Follow when I come out of the real estate office."

He went back, handing to the Brown Robin twenty-five dollars.

Finishing her business, she went out, followed by Mr. Cary. On the sidewalk she said:

"Now, Papa Cary, you must leave me. But you must come promptly when I send for you. Perhaps it will be to-morrow. Our fun is only beginning."

She asked Mr. Cary to stop a Lexington Avenue car for her and got aboard it when it came, bidding the elderly gentleman good-by at the car, very sweetly.

Mr. Cary, regaining the sidewalk, turned the corner, walking down Fourth Avenue to Twenty-second Street.

There he stopped, waiting for Chick and Patsy to come apace, and, when they did, he said:

"I want to get this makeup off as soon as I can."

"It's a pity to take it off," said Patsy. "It's great."

"Boys," said the elderly gentleman, "that woman is the Brown Robin."

"The devil!" exclaimed Patsy.

"I am the only detective, or police officer, that has ever spoken to the Brown Robin, knowing it to be her. I have her measure."

"Why didn't you nab her, then, chief?" asked Chick.

"Because she has worked the Cary matter so skillfully that I could not convict her. I want to get her foul on the Mountain case. But the Brown Robin is a woman."

"Then who the devil is Harold Stanton?" asked Patsy.

"I'll tell you that later. There are others, and we must capture them. But come with me."

They hurried to a neighboring hotel, where the Alpheus Cary who had dined with the Brown Robin quickly came out as Nick Carter, the famous detective.

CHAPTER VI.

AN AUDACIOUS VISITOR.

After he had removed his disguise, Nick said to his two aids:

"The Cary case will give us little trouble after this. I shall probably continue to play his part in it, but it will amount to little more than shelling out some money. She thinks she has captured him.

"She is a wonderfully clever woman, and is using the Cary incident merely as a cover to the big strike on Mountain.

"Now, Chick, tell me what you found in Seventeenth Street?"

"That the house was empty; that it had been occupied but two or three days; that the rent had been paid for a month; but possession has not been given up."

"Do you know who rented it?"

"A woman who gave the name of Mrs. Stanton."

"Hum! I fancy that she has rented another house this evening, the one in Thirtieth Street. In my way of thinking, that house is to be the scene of the strike on Mountain.

"That is a job for you, Patsy," continued Nick. "Watch that house from early to-morrow morning and settle who goes in and all about it. Nothing will be done there to-night.

"I must go to Cary's club and quiet him for the night. He is nearly in a collapse. How about Mountain, Chick?"

"I saw him. He is game, chief. Nothing came for him from the Brown Robin up to the time of his leaving his office. He will not yield. He is going to the theatre to-night."

"Do you know where?"

"Yes; at the Empire."

"Ah, ha! Be in the neighborhood, boys, and keep him under watch if you can. He is quite as likely to get his notice there as anywhere."

Nick went home satisfied that if there was any movement made that night, it would be only in the way he indicated.

"A lady is waiting to see you in the parlor, Nick," said Edith, as he entered.

"Who is it?"

"She would give no name," replied Edith. "She is young, pretty, and has asked me a lot of questions about you."

"Of course you gave me a good character," laughed Nick.

"I told the truth about you, and you can guess what it was, for I won't tell you," laughed Edith, in reply. "But hurry and get rid of her, for I want you to go out a ways with me."

Nick went to the parlor.

No man ever had a greater control of his features than the famous detective. He always maintained his self-control under the most trying circumstances. He had more than once looked certain death in the face without blinking.

But he had as narrow an escape from betraying himself as he ever met with, when, on opening the parlor door, he saw the Brown Robin occupying one of his sofas.

The shock was momentary and not observed by the other.

Nick crossed the room, bowing before his visitor, gravely, and said:

"I am Mr. Carter, madam."

The Brown Robin arose from her seat and looked most keenly and curiously into his face. Nick would have been dull indeed, if he had not also seen the look of admiration that grew on the face of his visitor.

But it did not affect him. Indeed he was just then striving to guess what the game of the Brown Robin was in seeking him at his own home.

"I should be much pleased, Mr. Carter," said the Brown Robin, "if you would listen to what I have to say and give me your advice."

"I certainly will listen to you," replied Nick, "but as to the advice I cannot tell yet. But, be seated and begin."

The Brown Robin sat down, and, taking from her pocket a letter, she said:

"If you will read that it will be a good beginning."

She handed it to him, and at a glance Nick saw that it was one of the kind with which now he was familiar. He read it:

"Mrs. Ansel:

"I have named my figures. I have only this to say further: If the money is not at the place to be mentioned, and at the time, your letters will be in the hands of your husband in the evening.

"The Brown Robin."

Nick handed the letter back and waited for the Brown Robin to speak. Apparently she was much embarrassed, and Nick, studying her, thought she was an admirable actress.

Finally she burst out:

"You are not at all sympathetic, Mr. Carter. Cannot you help me by asking questions?"

Nick smiled. Her acting pleased him, it was so good.

"I presume I can," he said. "I suppose this is a case of blackmail."

"Horrid blackmail."

"What are the letters referred to?"

"Mine, written before I was married."

"Why, then, should you fear to have your husband see them?"

"Well, they are compromising—that is, some of them—that is, in a way. They were written while I was engaged to the one who is now my husband, to a man of whom my husband is now and always has been desperately jealous."

"Who is this Brown Robin?"

"Don't you know?"

"I was asking if you knew."

"I only know that it is a name under which some one is making my life miserable. Who and what is the Brown Robin?"

"A blackmailer, evidently. I have heard of the name as used by a person in various cities, and latterly in New York."

"Is it a man or a woman?"

"The Brown Robin, I should judge, is a name used by a man and a woman, working together."

A faint smile flitted over the face of the lady.

There was a moment's silence. Then Nick asked:

"How did these letters get into the possession of the Brown Robin?"

"They were stolen from Mr. Collins."

"The man to whom they were written?"

"Yes."

"By whom?"

"By the Brown Robin, I suppose."

"How much money does she want?"

"One thousand dollars."

"And you cannot pay it?"

"I have no more money than my husband gives me, and he would find it difficult to raise so large a sum."

"Now, then, what is it you wish from me?"

"Well, what am I to do?"

"I think I should say that it is simply impossible—that you would find it difficult to raise a thousand cents. Convince these people of your inability to raise the money, and, as a rule, they drop the thing. It is the hope of getting money that makes them hold on."

"But cannot you give me some way of getting back those letters?"

"Frankly, Mrs. Ansel, for that I take to be your name," said Nick, "I don't think the game is worth the candle.

"If I were in your place, I should take a detective of the regular force with me to the appointed place, and when the blackmailer appeared, put him, or her, or them, under arrest. They would give up the letters to be released."

"Wouldn't you go with me?"

Immediately Nick thought he saw through the purpose of the call. It was the audacious effort of which he had spoken to Edith, of leading him into a compromising trap.

It did not anger him, for he rather admired the boldness and audacity of it.

However, his first impulse was to refuse, but his second thought was to see it out. He said:

"I am a very busy man just now, and cannot control my time. What is the hour of this meeting, and where is it to be?"

"The hour is eleven to-morrow, but I am to be informed early to-morrow morning of the place."

"Very well, I will go with you, if you inform me early enough."

The Brown Robin arose, apparently much pleased with the success of her visit, and shortly after left.

Nick went back to Edith, telling her to prepare herself for her walk and saying that he wanted to go in the neighborhood of the Festus Club, for a moment's word with one of his clients.

When she came back, ready for her walk, she asked:

"Who was your caller, Nick?"

"The Brown Robin."

"Nick! You don't mean that that pretty woman is the Brown Robin?"

"No doubt of it!"

"How do you know?"

"I called on the Brown Robin to-day, disguised as Alpheus Cary."

"And she had the audacity to come and see you, knowing you are retained to expose her?"

"Boldness and audacity are her weapons."

"What did she want?"

"She pretended that she was a Mrs. Ansel, who was being blackmailed by the Brown Robin."

"She came to measure you, Nick, to size you up, as you call it."

"Perhaps that was her game. She has never seen me, I suppose. But, Edith, I think she was laying the trap of which I spoke this morning."

"How?"

"She wanted me to accompany her as Mrs. Ansel to meet the Brown Robin and compel the giving up of the letters."

"Ah! and you do not walk into the trap."

"But I will. Something of value may come out of it. I will escape it, never fear. Chick and Patsy will not be far off, I can tell you."

Edith made no reply. Quite evidently she did not like it, but she knew it was useless to combat Nick when he had made up his mind.

So she held her peace and went out for her walk with him.

During their walk they stopped at the door of the Festus Club, where Nick told Mr. Cary that he had his case so well in hand that the old gentleman could go home and sleep in comfort.

CHAPTER VII.

CHICK'S GREAT DISCOVERY.

When Nick had left Chick and Patsy at the hotel, where he had taken off the disguise of Mr. Cary, the two young detectives discussed their own details for the night.

"We're to keep a watch over Mountain," said Chick.

"He seems able to watch over himself," replied Patsy.

"Oh, he's able enough," said Chick. "It isn't that. The chief wants to know the moment he gets the word from the Brown Robin. He believes that the Brown Robin will show up to-night."

"Then we must be on," said Patsy. "It's up to us to decorate the lobby of the Empire with our beauty. Say, Chick, it's the old story. We've swung about the Tenderloin so much lately that too many know us."

"And we'll have to look different. Well, Patsy, let's swing out as swell Willie boys."

Patsy laughed heartily, pounding the pillar against which he had been leaning.

"A sweet Willie boy you'll make Chick," he said, after a while, "with those broad shoulders of yours. No, no, Chick. Do your own act. Swing out as a regular swell."

Chick looked at his watch, and said:

"It is nearly time to rig, then. But come with me first. I want to look over that Seventeenth Street house again. Though the people in the neighborhood say the folks who were in it for three days have left it, I've a notion it's still in the game."

The two moved off in the direction of the house in question, and had reached the corner of Twenty-third Street and Lexington Avenue on their way, when a young man in a blue flannel shirt and a coil of wire about his shoulder, stopped Chick and asked:

"Ain't you Chickering Carter?"

"Yes," replied Chick, eying the young man keenly.

"Well, say," said the young man, "it's up to me to tell you something. Say, I've been chewing on it all day, and just as soon as I was cleaned up

I was going to hunt up Nick Carter and give it away, if it did fling me out of a job."

"Can you tell me?" asked Chick.

"That's what I hollered whoa on you for. You'll do just as well."

"Step aside, then," said Chick.

Chick led the way to a place near the corner, where they could talk unobserved, followed by both Patsy and the young man.

"Now, then, what is it?" asked Chick

"I've been dead wrong," said the young man, "and I'm going to square it, even if you fling me over to the company. It's this way. I'm lineman for the telephone company. See?

"I know all about Nick Carter, and you, and Patsy and Ida. See? Well, I was working on the line up by Ida's house this morning, where a break had been reported, and I had to go on to the top of a house right by hers.

"Well, I found a wire had been rung in on it, and I followed it to see that it run over the gutter and to a window on the third floor. See?

"I went down to that room, and there was a young woman, and she was a peach, all smiles. See?

"'You've found it,' she says, 'and caught me. Now don't give me away, 'cause there's nothing in it. I was only trying to get on to my best feller.' See?

"Anyhow, she give me the great jolly and I went in up to my neck. I was soft as butter. When she flung up a fiver at me, hanged if I didn't do what she wanted, and fixed the wire to an old 'phone she had in the room.

"She jollied me into it. See? After I got away from her, I began to think, and the more I thought the more wrong it was to me, and I saw what mush I'd been in the hands of a pretty woman.

"So, after I'd been thinking an hour, I went back to unfix it. Say! Just as I got to her door I heard her say: 'All right, chief, this is Ida.' Then I took a big tumble. I listened and heard her say over what the one at the other end had been saying, something about 'Herman Hartwig' and 'Passen.' She had got on to Nick Carter's talk and was a crook playing Ida.

"I took a sneak up to the roof, cut the leak wire, and switched the other over so that the crook couldn't get at it again.

"That's all there is of it. I've squared it with you, and, if you want to, you can report me to the company and get me sacked. I won't squeal."

"Well," cried Chick, "I wouldn't do that, anyway. And now that you've squared yourself this way, I wouldn't think of it.

"It was the chief she was talking with over the wire, but there wasn't any harm done, for he dropped right away that it wasn't Ida on the other end, and gave the other a throw-off. He cut the connections with his own 'phone.

"If you want to square it right with the chief, go to his place to-morrow morning and put the connections on. I'll see him to-night and square you with him."

The young man, expressing satisfaction with this arrangement, went off, after shaking hands with both Chick and Patsy.

But he had gotten no farther than the corner when he stopped short, peered forward eagerly, and came back to the young detectives on a run.

"Say," he cried. "Come. The young woman is going down the av'noo. Sure, it's her."

"Who?" asked Patsy.

"The one who worked me on the wires."

The two followed quickly to the corner, where the man pointed out a woman moving along at a brisk gait down Lexington Avenue.

"Come on, Patsy," cried Chick.

The young man evidently thought he was in it, too, for he followed after.

The woman, plainly unconscious that she was followed, went on until she reached Twenty-first Street, when she was stopped by Grammery Park.

She turned to the right, or toward the west, and went around the park to Twentieth Street, and so down to Irving place.

Into this short street she turned, continuing on to Seventeenth Street.

"Hide!" cried Chick, just as she reached the corner, springing over the fence into a courtyard.

Patsy obeyed immediately and the lineman caught on quickly enough to prevent himself from being seen.

As Chick had anticipated, the woman had stood still on the corner and looked back.

As no one was to be seen, she was apparently satisfied that she was unobserved, for she turned to the left and went out of sight.

The three came from their hiding places, and, at Chick's suggestion, Patsy stole up to the corner, peering around it.

He signaled for Chick to come, and dashed across Seventeenth Street.

The woman was pursuing her way toward Third Avenue on the upper side of Seventeenth Street.

"Keep back, out of sight," said Chick to the lineman.

The young man fell back, and Chick advanced cautiously, taking advantage of every obstruction of which he could make use.

Patsy was pursuing the same tactics on the other side of the street.

When within a few doors of Third Avenue, the woman again stopped and looked back.

This had been anticipated by Chick, too, and he was out of sight when she turned.

Nor was Patsy to be seen. The only one in the vista was a man—the lineman—and his back was turned, as if he were walking toward Irving Place.

Hastily she ran up the steps of the house in front of which she had stopped, and disappeared through the door.

Chick and Patsy both appeared at the same instant. Chick sounded a signal, and Patsy came running to him.

"Is it the house, Chick?" he asked.

"The same one, Patsy," replied Chick.

"Then it is the Brown Robin."

"Perhaps. We'll pipe off the house for a while."

The lineman came back to them, and learning what they were about to do, concluded to go off, but Chick persuaded him to stay.

While he had every reason to believe that the young fellow was honest, yet he would not take the chance of having him give warning.

The wait was half an hour in length, during which time the three were completely concealed under the areaway of a vacant house.

About the time that Patsy expressed the opinion that the woman was settled for the night, a form was seen to appear on the stoop from within the house they were watching.

"Here she comes!" cried Patsy.

The figure descended the steps.

"It's a man," said the lineman, "not a woman."

The figure turned from the house toward the west, approaching closely to the spot where the three were hidden.

As the man passed them, the light of a street lamp fell upon him.

Patsy caught the arm of Chick in a firm grip, and held it until the figure of the man passed far enough along to be beyond the possibility of hearing.

"It is the one I followed this morning," he whispered.

"The deuce!" exclaimed Chick. "The one who wrote the letter—who went to sleep in the hotel?"

"Yes; in the disguise he put on after he ran away from the insurance building."

"Get out and watch him," said Chick to the lineman.

The young fellow did as he was told, and presently reported that the man was crossing Irving Place and going up Seventeenth Street to the west.

"Patsy," said Chick, "go and rig yourself for the night's work. I'll take up the shadow and will give you the trail."

Patsy was about to go off, but he waited to hear Chick say to the lineman:

"It isn't worth your while to follow us longer."

But at the moment the lineman said:

"The fellow is coming back."

Again the three went into hiding to see that the young fellow stopped at the corner of Irving Place.

He stood there a moment or two, looking down the street, and passed out of sight.

Patsy stole up to the corner, and lightly leaping into the courtyard of the house on the corner, threw himself on the ground and wriggled to the corner, to see the man standing nearby, leaning against the fence.

Patsy wriggled back, and signaled to Chick that the man was there yet.

Chick gave the return signal to keep up the watch, and himself stole down the street to the house whence the man had come.

Looking up at it, there were no indications that it was occupied.

Pulling from his pocket a false mustache and a wig, he donned them quickly, keenly alive to any signal Patsy might give, and, mounting the steps, rang the bell.

Chick had a notion in his head that he wanted to satisfy.

There was no response, though he rang several times.

Then he tried the outer door. It opened to him, and he found himself in a vestibule. The inner doors were locked.

He picked the lock quickly and stepped into a dark hall. There were no signs or sounds of life within the house, but all was darkness.

Chick drew his revolver, and then took from his coat pocket his lantern.

Feeling for the parlor door, he entered that room and listened. Then he flashed his lantern. It was empty. By the light he located the stairs, and shutting it off, cautiously climbed them to the second floor, where he listened again.

There was no sound of anything. Again flashing his light, he found an open door in front of him.

He entered. On the bed was a lot of women's clothes. He examined them. It was a complete woman's costume.

On a chair was some men's apparel.

Chick went back to the woman's clothes and muttered:

"It is just what I thought."

He gave a hasty glance at the bureau. On it was a lot of paint and cosmetic; several false beards, mustaches and wigs.

"I've got this for a certainty."

He bounded out of the room, going hurriedly into every part of the house. It was empty; not a soul in it.

He went to the front door, and as he did so he heard some one on the outside.

He darted into the parlor and not a moment too soon, for some one entered and hastily ran upstairs in the dark.

Quick as a flash and as a light shone forth on the second floor, Chick slipped out of the front doors and down the steps.

Reaching the sidewalk, he sounded a low whistle.

Promptly came the response; Chick bounded in its direction.

Patsy appeared from under a stoop; Chick went to him.

"Who went into that house?" he asked.

"The same one who came out. He came back all of a sudden, as if he had just thought of something, nearly catching me. Who came out just now?"

"I did."

"The devil!"

"Yes; I've been through the house. There wasn't a soul in it."

"But the woman who went in?"

"Patsy, I've tumbled to a big thing. The woman who went in and the man who came out are the same person. But hurry off, Patsy, rig up and find my trail. There's business on hand."

Patsy dashed away and was hardly out of sight, when Chick saw the young man come from the house and hurriedly pass up Seventeenth Street.

Chick was after him quickly, a piece of red chalk in his hand. The lineman had disappeared.

CHAPTER VIII.

A DEEP GAME.

For some time, as a matter of convenience for making changes and as a meeting place for himself and aids, Nick had maintained a room in the hotel where, in the late afternoon of the day in which these events took place, he had taken off his makeup as Mr. Cary.

It was to this place that Patsy hurried to make the change that would prevent him from being recognized by the Brown Robin.

It did not take him long, and when he turned out into the street again, in his dress suit and mustache, he looked like a veritable young man about town—a handsome swell.

He had supposed when he left the room where he made the change that he would have to return to the neighborhood where Chick had made his great discovery, to pick up Chick's trail.

But he had barely stepped through the main entrance to the hotel when he saw, on the pavement directly in front, a roughly-drawn arrow in red chalk, the head pointing to the north.

It was Chick's trail.

"Great luck!" exclaimed Patsy to himself, as he hurried up to the corner. "I'm on as the flag falls."

At the corner the sign showed that Chick had crossed the street to the west side of Broadway, but on reaching the corner on that side, Patsy could see nothing that indicated further direction.

"Great Scott!" exclaimed Patsy. "They have taken a car."

He went back to the middle of the street, and, looking about carefully, saw some pieces of paper.

He looked for a trail of them, but the wind had evidently blown them away.

Searching further, Patsy's eye was caught by an upright form which fluttered a small red flag, a signal of some kind, used in the operation of the street railway.

This upright was a slender rod of iron, but about it was tied a small bit of red cloth.

Patsy went to it, to recognize it as one of Chick's signs.

A railroad man came up, warning Patsy away from the signal.

"Now, who the deuce did that?" he exclaimed, tearing off Chick's signal.

But Patsy had seen it, and knew that Chick had taken an upbound car.

So he mounted the next one, quite certain that Chick's destination was the Empire Theatre.

But, all the same, he kept a sharp lookout for any signal that might have been left by Chick on the way.

He saw none, however, until in passing the Empire Theatre, his eye caught a strip of red cloth, a foot long, fluttering from the billboard of the theatre.

"Chick's there," he muttered.

At Fortieth Street he got out and walked back to the theatre, taking off the strip of cloth which had been fastened by a pin, as he entered, placing it in his pocket.

As he entered the lobby, a man in ordinary clothes passed out, making a signal to Patsy.

Even before Patsy saw the signal he had recognized Chick, though he was disguised by a false mustache and wig.

He followed Chick out, and when he came up, Chick said:

"My man, who is a woman—the Brown Robin—is in there, looking at the play. The second act is on.

"Mountain is in there, too. The Brown Robin talked with Mountain after the first act. What was said between them I don't know, but whatever it was, the Brown Robin asked something from Mountain which he refused to give or do.

"I couldn't get to him before he went back to his seat."

"Catch him after this act," said Patsy.

"That's what I want to do," said Chick, "and I have been thinking it over and how to do it. You see, if we talk with Mountain in the open, the Brown Robin will drop, and that is what we don't want.

"Say, Patsy, you know the manager, don't you?"

"Yes; he's all right—nice fellow."

"Well, can't you see him now, and ask him to let us into a room and send for Mr. Mountain?"

"Sure."

Patsy went off, and in a few moments was back again, saying it was all arranged. He led Chick into a room opening off the lobby, and when the door was closed Patsy laughed and said:

"This job was easy enough, Chick, but the hard part was to convince our friend that I was the one I said I was. He knows Mountain, so that is all right."

At this moment the door opened, and a short, rather stout man, with a sharp, bright, masterful face, entered, looking keenly about.

"The great mogul over all here," whispered Patsy.

It was indeed the great theatrical manager of the day.

"Which one is Patsy?" he asked.

Patsy stood up, and the great manager looked him over keenly.

Then he laughed heartily, and shook hands with the lad.

"Patsy," he said, "I think I shall have to engage you to teach makeup to my young people. Yours is a triumph of art."

Directing the boy in attendance to make the two comfortable, he went out.

Shortly after, a bell sounded in the room.

"The act is over," said Chick; "now for Mountain."

They did not wait long, for the door soon opened and Mr. Mountain, in evening attire, entered.

He looked at the two with the air of one who had expected to find acquaintances and had met strangers.

"Mr. Mountain," said Chick, "we are two of Nick Carter's men."

"The woods are full of them, then," said Mr. Mountain, seriously, "for this is the second time I have been accosted by them."

"Do you mean," asked Chick, "that the one who spoke to you after the first act said he was one of Nick Carter's men?"

"That's what he did."

"For Heaven's sake!" exclaimed Chick. "I hope you gave him no confidence."

"I did not. I told him that I did not know whether he was or not, and I would not talk to him until I knew or he proved it. Then I told him that when I knew him to be one of Nick Carter's men I would have nothing to do with him, or Nick Carter, either, for I had been warned against all. And that's what I say to you."

"You do not recognize me, then, Mr. Mountain?"

"I do not."

Chick stood up, and quickly removed his mustache and wig.

"How now, Mr. Mountain?"

"There's no doubt of it now," laughed Mr. Mountain.

"I am Patsy, Mr. Mountain," said the lad, "but I can't take off my makeup so quickly or put it on again."

"Well, boys," said Mr. Mountain, "what's in the wind?"

"We have been detailed by the chief to watch over you, Mr. Mountain," said Chick. "He had a notion that you would get your notice tonight."

"He was right. I did."

"When?"

"See here, Chick," said Mr. Mountain, "Carter told me that if I was questioned I must deny having anything to do with him or his men."

"That's all right, Mr. Mountain," said Chick. "The chief has a notion that they do not know that you have retained him, and he wants to keep the thing quiet. I hope you did not let on to that young man that you had relations with us."

"Why?"

"Because that was the Brown Robin."

"The devil! I saw Nick Carter only a couple of hours ago, and he told me the Brown Robin was a woman."

"The person speaking to you after the first act was a woman."

"What? Are you sure?"

"Certain. Now, then, what did she want?"

"Say, Chick," exclaimed Patsy. "Hold on! Mr. Mountain has seen her in the makeup she had when she left Seventeenth Street."

"That's all right, Patsy, but she made a change on her way up here. Now, Mr. Mountain, what did she want?"

"Well, after telling me she was one of Nick Carter's men, she asked if I had got my notice. I refused to say anything to her on the subject, and when she talked Nick Carter I told her, as Mr. Carter had instructed me, that I had nothing to do with him, and wanted to have nothing to do.

"He—that is, she, if it is a she—began to threaten me with Nick Carter's power, but I wouldn't have it. I stood pat on Mr. Carter's instructions."

"That is first-rate," said Chick. "I see the game through and through. It was an effort to be satisfied whether or not Nick Carter is employed by you."

"Well, then, she is satisfied that he is not, for I lied like a trooper."

"Good! Now, then, you have got your notice?"

"Yes."

"How?"

"By letter. It was thrust into my hand as I entered the theatre here."

"May I see it?"

Mr. Mountain took a letter from his pocket, handing it to Chick, who, after reading it, passed it to Patsy. It read:

"Mr. M.:

"Tomorrow at 5 P. M. Be at the entrance of the Park Avenue Hotel, prepared to do business, as I require. Make no mistake as to the amount. You will be met by one who will bring you to me. If you are accompanied by any one, or, if any one is concealed there to watch and follow, I shall know it, and if you play tricks the game will be up. Be prompt.

"The Brown Robin."

"So it's business tomorrow," said Chick.

"It seems so," replied Mr. Mountain. "I want to see Carter on this business; I meant to go to him after the theatre."

"Don't; let him go to you," said Chick. "You will be seen and followed if you go. He will get to you unseen."

"I suppose that is so," said Mr. Mountain, thoughtfully. "You will inform him then?"

"Yes; I will take this letter to him."

Chick was thoughtful a moment, then handed the letter back, saying:

"On second thoughts, Mr. Mountain, keep that letter in your pocket. You may be required to show it, and it may be well to do it, if so."

"How?"

"The man who first came to you may show up before the evening is over."

"I see."

"A lot may be done to find out whether you are acting in good faith before they put their heads in the trap."

"I follow you. Good! I am to act as I meant to come down in earnest."

"That is it."

The bell sounded again to notify of the raising of the curtain.

"Go back, Mr. Mountain, as if nothing had occurred here," said Chick.

Mr. Mountain went into the lobby, and Chick asked an attendant if there was a way out of the room except through the lobby.

An unknown way was pointed out, and through it Chick and Patsy went out to Broadway.

Here Chick said:

"Now, Patsy, go into the theatre and keep up the watch. I think Mountain will be shadowed home; follow if he is. I shall hunt up the chief."

Patsy obeyed, and went into the theatre, paying his admission, to see the man he had followed earlier in the day, in the same disguise in which he had come from the Seventeenth Street house; that is to say, the Brown Robin, standing just within the audience hall.

He took up a standing position near her.

Chick hurried across town to Nick's apartments and arrived a few minutes after Nick had returned from his walk with Edith.

The famous detective listened intently to what Chick had to tell.

"This is great work of yours, Chick," he said. "You have proved satisfactorily what I have suspected ever since I was at the Brown Robin's house as Mr. Cary.

"The suspicion that the man that followed me this morning and was followed by Patsy afterward was a woman came to me when he took me to the Lexington house."

"I was looking for the knock-kneed gait that the keen-witted Patsy spoke of, and then it struck me it was a woman, well padded and made up."

"But, chief, you saw the man go out of the Lexington Avenue house just as the Brown Robin came to you."

"No, I didn't, Chick," replied Nick, with a smile. "I heard it. But I dropped then, or thought I did, that the two voices were from the same person—a little play played for my benefit.

"She is a great actress, Chick, and a thundering smart woman. She has the energy of the devil. When she left me, as Mr. Cary, in Twenty-third Street, she must have come straight over here. Leaving here, she made for the Seventeenth Street house, to make her change for the night's work.

"That was a great piece of work of yours to go into that house. It proved the fact, and shows up her game.

"I can see now how she baffled all the others. She has three houses to work in, and in the Lexington Avenue house she is seen only as a woman, except as she ordered it today.

"She is great on makeup, and she plays the game herself. Well, she makes the big strike tomorrow, and we'll have her.

"We'll meet her with her own cunning.

"But come, we'll go to Mr. Mountain's house, to be there before he gets back from the theatre.

"Take my word for it, Chick, the Thirtieth Street house is to be the scene of the big strike."

With this, the two detectives set out for Mr. Mountain's residence.

CHAPTER IX.

THE TRAP.

Patsy arrived early the next morning to report to Nick that on the night previous the Brown Robin, still in male attire, had followed Mr. Mountain to his home, after that gentleman had left the theatre with his family.

She had been around the front of the house for some little time, and then, as if satisfied that Mr. Mountain was housed for the night, had left, going directly to the corner of Thirty-fourth Street and Sixth Avenue, where she met two men, evidently awaiting her coming.

Only a word or two was exchanged between them, and they then set off at a quick pace, going straight to the Thirtieth Street house, where the Brown Robin had unlocked the doors and let the two men in.

She did not enter the house herself, but now hurried to Lexington Avenue, where she took the car, getting off at Twenty-third Street, and going to the Seventeenth Street house, which she entered some time after midnight.

She was there but a short time, when she came out clad in woman's clothes, and went straight to the Lexington Avenue house, evidently her day's work done.

"Well," said Nick, "it was a hard day's work, and she filled in all her time.

"She was arranging her programme for tomorrow. We have arranged our programme, too. Those two men that she let into the Thirtieth Street house are there to help her in the strike on Mr. Mountain.

"I doubt if there will be any others on hand. You need not watch it this morning. My plans have been slightly changed since my talk with Mr. Mountain last night.

"But I want you to put yourself in a place outside where you can follow me this morning when I go out: I suppose the Brown Robin will try to spring her trap on me this morning."

Patsy had been gone but a few moments when a messenger boy arrived with a letter for Nick.

It was signed by Mrs. Ansel, and said that the place appointed for her in which to meet the Brown Robin was in Seventeenth Street at eleven o'clock, and it asked if Mr. Carter would meet the writer at a well-known department store in Sixth Avenue at 10 A. M., naming the entrance at which Mrs. Ansel would be waiting.

Nick carefully examined the letter and noted several things. The stationery was not the same as that which had been used for the former letters; the handwriting was not the same, and the letter was framed so skillfully that it was made to look like the letter of a woman asking an assignation with a man.

Nick called Edith and asked her to read the letter. As Edith was doing so he took some papers from his pocket, and from these selected a blank sheet and an envelope.

"Compare this blank paper and the paper on which this note is written," said Nick.

"It is the same," said Edith.

"Even the most cunning make their slips," said Nick. "I found this blank paper on a table in the parlor of the Brown Robin in Lexington Avenue, as I did also a sheet of the other paper. Keep them, and the letter as well.

"I am off to meet this very cunning person and see what her little game is. I confess I can't quite see through it."

He went away, and promptly at ten appeared at the entrance of the department store named.

The Brown Robin was waiting, and, as he approached, Nick did not fail to observe a flash of triumph in the eyes of that person.

She arose to meet him, and welcomed him cordially.

"I was very much afraid that you would fail me," she said.

"Oh, no," he said, carelessly. "I am quite anxious to see this Brown Robin."

"Why, indeed!"

"She must be an attractive person. An old gentleman who ought to know better was caught by her, and rushed off to me to get him out of his trouble. But before I could get to work, he backed out of the matter, and, I think, because she has entangled him in her charms."

The one beside him looked up quickly at Nick, but she could not read his face.

"They say," said she, "that there is no fool like an old fool. I suppose you could not be caught that way."

"A man is very foolish to boast of his ability to resist the charms of a pretty woman," said Nick, gravely. "I have seen too many strong men caught to be boastful myself."

"Perhaps it is the story of her charms that makes you so willing to go with me?"

"Perhaps," replied Nick, "but I think it is more out of curiosity to see the woman who has baffled the police forces of so many large cities. It might be useful, you know, to me some time. There's no knowing how soon a case in which she is operating may be given me."

To this the pretended Mrs. Ansel made no reply.

After a moment Nick said:

"Ought we not to go?"

"As it draws near to the time, I am a little frightened," she said.

Nevertheless she made preparations to start.

They went out of the store, walking down Sixth Avenue to Eighteenth Street, and then through that street to Fifth Avenue.

On the corner of that street the pretended Mrs. Ansel suddenly gave a little scream, clung tightly to Nick for a moment, and then leaped into a doorway, hiding herself.

Nick did not follow her, but stood still, watching her. The woman peered out cautiously; finally she came with a greatly frightened air to him, gasping out:

"My husband! He just crossed the street."

"What then?" asked Nick.

"Oh, if he had seen you with me there would have been such a row. He is so jealous—so suspicious!"

"Come along and point him out to me."

He fairly pulled her to the corner, but, reaching it, the pretended Mrs. Ansel could not see her husband.

"That frightens me," she said. "He may have seen me. He may be hiding to watch me. Oh, come away!"

She hurried across the street, Nick following her.

From that time on she kept up her nervous, frightened manner, until the door of the Seventeenth Street house was reached.

"What an admirable actress she is!" thought Nick. "She is wasting great talents in a dangerous game when she might win fame on the stage."

At this house, looking up at the number, she said:

"This is the place. Shall we go in?"

"That is what we came for, isn't it?" asked Nick.

Without another word, the pretended Mrs. Ansel mounted the steps and rang the bell. Nick followed her up leisurely.

The door was opened promptly by a large, stalwart woman dressed as a servant.

To this person the pretended Mrs. Ansel said:

"Mrs. Ansel and Mr. Nicholas Carter, to see the person named on this."

She handed a small slip of paper to the servant.

The servant closed the door and ushered them into the parlor, going out into another part of the house.

She was back again in a few moments to say that the lady of the house was engaged for the present, but would see them shortly.

Nick said to himself:

"All this is well done, but what is the game?"

In the meantime the pretended Mrs. Ansel showed every evidence of the natural nervousness that a woman placed in the position she pretended to be in might show.

Nick had seated himself at a little distance from her, but shortly she beckoned him to a seat beside her on the sofa.

"I don't think I can stand this suspense," she said. "It is all I can do to keep from fainting."

And no sooner had she said this than she reeled over, falling completely into Nick's arms.

At that very moment, a man whose face was blazing with anger, rushed into the room, crying:

"So, I have tracked you at last. I have you with your paramour, in fact. You wretch!"

To all appearances the woman had fainted dead away and did not hear the angry words.

Nick lifted her up and laid her on the sofa where she lay as he put her, and stood up.

"Who are you?" asked Nick.

"Who am I?" repeated the other. "The deceived husband."

"Is your name Ansel?"

"Yes. I am the husband of that wretched woman."

"Well, is the fact that a woman faints evidence against her?"

"Don't trifle with me, sir. I have followed you here. I knew she had an appointment with some one this morning. I watched and have found her in her guilt."

"In the house of the blackmailer known as the Brown Robin?" sneered Nick.

At this moment the pretended Mrs. Ansel opened her eyes, started up, and cried out:

"My husband! I am ruined!"

Again she toppled off into a faint.

"I suppose this is a well-worked game?" said Nick. "Well, play it to the end. How much do you want? Make it as easy as you can. I can't afford much, but I can't afford a scandal about my name."

As he said this, Nick carefully watched the Brown Robin, and was certain he saw first a look of surprise and then of triumph on what was supposed to be an unconscious face.

"Money," cried the man, "I want no money. Would money restore my wretched home, my happiness, the mother of my children?"

Nick could hardly restrain a smile, for the man was clearly over-acting. But Nick kept up the pretense, for he wanted to see where the game was to lead to.

"No; but you shall sign a confession. You shall give me the proof. You shall give me the means of tearing asunder these bonds that have now become hateful to me.

"Here, sign this!"

He drew a paper from his pocket, and, spreading it on a table, gestured in the most melodramatic manner to Nick to sign it.

Nick crossed the room and took up the paper.

As he lifted it to read he saw that the pretended Mrs. Ansel had recovered consciousness, and was sitting upright on the sofa.

As soon as she saw Nick had observed her, she began to play her part.

"Oh, my husband!" she cried; "be merciful. I know appearances are against me, but you are mistaken. I have done no wrong. Listen to reason. This is not a lover. It is Mr. Carter, the great detective."

"I care not who he is," cried the other, in a great pretense of fury. "You met him by appointment. I watched you send the letter. I saw him meet you. I tracked you here. I saw you in his arms. I have witnesses. Sign you, sir!"

It was very cheap acting, but through it all Nick had read the paper, and saw that it was an effort to make him compromise himself by signing it.

"I shall sign nothing of this kind!" he said, quietly.

"You won't. You won't give me justice!" cried the man, in a very tempest of fury.

"I won't sign this ridiculous document," said Nick, "for it is not true."

"Then I will take action at once. You must stay here. What, ho, my friends!"

Three men, thorough ruffians, looking like dissipated prize-fighters, appeared.

"You will watch this man until I return. I go for my lawyer and a magistrate. Hold this man until I return. Come with me, you faithless woman!"

He sprang at the pretended Mrs. Ansel, and, seizing her by the arm, whirled her out of the room.

CHAPTER X.

HOW THE TRAP WAS SPRUNG.

Nick sat down and laughed. The over-acting of the cheap actor, hired for the occasion, was ludicrous. But the three ruffians, armed with revolvers, were ugly facts.

He now saw the game. The trap had been sprung. It was a device to get him under control while the big strike on Mountain was being worked.

Either the Brown Robin feared he had been retained by Mr. Mountain, or she had learned, despite his efforts to the contrary, that he really had been.

"Well," he said, looking at the three brutes, "what is your game?"

"To keep you here all day," replied one of them.

"Oh, is it?" asked Nick. "What has become of the woman that was here?"

"She has gone out with her husband."

"Oh, drop that, my lads," said Nick. "That was the Brown Robin. I knew that when I came in here with her."

The three men grinned, and one said to the other:

"I told her she couldn't fool him."

"I suppose you mean to earn your money by keeping me here?" said Nick.

"Yer right, guv-ner."

"Well, I don't know that I can blame you," said Nick, "but I want to know for sure that the woman is gone."

"She's gone, all right."

"Well, take me through the house, and let me be certain."

"There can't be any harm in that," said one. "Go ahead quietly, me and Smithy'll go behind."

Thus escorted, Nick went through and made sure the Brown Robin had fled the house.

After all, it was a vulgar trap which had been laid for him.

He returned to the parlors and sat down a while. Then he asked one of the men to open a window and let a little air in.

When this was done, he took some cigars from his pocket and handed them to his guards.

Then he went to the piano, and, seating himself, to the great pleasure of the three brutes, he sang:

> *"Come to me, darling, I'm lonely without thee,*
> *Daytime and nighttime I'm dreaming about thee."*

He knew Patsy, and probably Chick, were without and would take his song as a call for them.

Nor was he mistaken. But a few minutes passed when his quick ears heard a sound at the front door that told him the lock was being picked.

Again he seated himself at the piano, and began to sing and play. The brutes were attentive upon him.

But, through the corner of his eye, he saw Chick at the hall door.

Wheeling about on the piano stool, he sprang to his feet, and, drawing his revolver, cried out:

"Down, you dogs!"

Chick sprang into the room from the front door and Patsy came in from the rear room, revolvers up.

The brutes, taken by astonishment, could not rally in time, and, seeing they were powerless, threw up their hands.

"Take their guns, Patsy," said Nick.

This the lad quickly did, while Nick and Chick covered them.

"Boys," said Nick, "I'm sorry to treat you so, but I must. You must be bound and gagged, but I'll let you loose in time."

The three did not dare to make resistance, and, making them as comfortable as circumstances would permit, the three detectives took care to carefully lock the house up. Then they quietly departed.

"It was a stupid way," said Nick to Patsy and Chick, as they walked away, "and more like a cheap melodrama than anything else. Really, I believe the Brown Robin has been an actress some time in her life."

* * * *

Shortly before five o'clock that afternoon Mr. Mountain, with a small package under his arm, appeared on the steps of the Park Avenue Hotel.

He had not been there long before the young man who had first called on him came up.

It was, of course, the Brown Robin. Her tactics were precisely the same as they had been with Mr. Cary the day before, that is, with Nick disguised as Mr. Cary.

And the same questions were put to him as to any person being in concealment.

When these had been answered as the person desired, Mr. Mountain was asked if he was ready to go and see the Brown Robin.

"Yes," replied Mr. Mountain, "if it is to be done, let us do it right away. But first let me go into the hotel with this."

The young man was reluctant, but yet he followed and Mr. Mountain, going to the desk, asked the clerk to place it in the safe and give it to no one but himself.

This done, the two walked out of the hotel.

As Nick had foreseen, their way was up to the Thirtieth Street house. What the young man did not see was a trick played by Mr. Mountain, a trick taught him by Nick.

Every three or four steps they took, a small piece of paper fluttered from Mr. Mountain's hand. It was thus Nick could ascertain that the Thirtieth Street house was their destination.

Everything moved precisely as it had the day before. The young man showed Mr. Mountain into the parlor and disappeared to call the person Mr. Mountain had come to see.

There was a wait for some time, and then the Brown Robin swept into the room.

"I am very glad to renew your acquaintance, Mr. Mountain," said the Brown Robin.

Mr. Mountain fairly staggered in his surprise.

"Why! Why!" he exclaimed. "Alberta Curtis!"

"The same," said the Brown Robin. "Although I have had many experiences since I was your typewriter, my name has remained the same through it all."

"Then it was you, after all, that stole the confession," blurted out Mr. Mountain.

"Stole is an ugly word, my dear old employer," said the Brown Robin. "Be more polite. Say I confiscated it when I found it among loose papers."

Mr. Mountain, though he had suspected this, yet, when he learned that it was so, seemed amazed and stupefied.

But the Brown Robin soon brought him to his senses by asking if he had come to do business.

In her dealings with Mr. Mountain, there was none of the coquetry she had displayed with Mr. Cary.

Thus aroused, Mr. Mountain said:

"Your terms are outrageous!"

"Let us be plain and brief, Mr. Mountain. You have become a very rich man. Fifty thousand dollars will not even embarrass you. I have informed myself exactly as to your financial condition.

"You can afford to pay that to preserve your good name and your reputation.

"Now, read this."

She took from her pocket a typewritten roll of paper, and extended it to Mr. Mountain.

"You will see that it is a carefully-prepared newspaper article, which embraces your confession.

"If you refuse to pay what I believe is the value of that confession, in your handwriting, to you, that will be published."

Mr. Mountain read it over, and saw with what skill it was prepared, and how eagerly a paper would seize on it.

"You would not have the cruelty to do that?"

"You are mistaken," said the Brown Robin, coldly. "I would have and will do what I say I will. Make not the least mistake about that."

"But you will do it for less?"

"Fifty thousand or nothing."

This was said with the utmost firmness. Then she added:

"But why shuffle? The very fact you are here shows that you are here to comply."

"I am to have the original confession for that payment?"

"Yes."

"Must I trust to your honor to get it?"

"Show me the money and I will show you the document."

"Very well."

"Understand," said the Brown Robin. "I am well guarded. I can defend myself with this."

She displayed a revolver.

"I stand on a push-button," she went on, "and the slightest pressure will summon to my aid, if you attempt any tricks, those who will defend me."

"Very good!"

Mr. Mountain placed his hand in his pocket, and, taking out an envelope, took out a check, holding it in his hand.

The Brown Robin, in the act of drawing a paper from the breast of her dress, stopped.

"A check! Is this a trick, or is it your ignorance?"

"Why, yes, a check drawn to my own order for fifty thousand dollars, and indorsed by me. You did not tell me in what shape you wanted it."

"True. But you must have understood."

Suddenly she flew into a violent passion, in which she declared that she would ruin him, really frightening Mr. Mountain.

He tried to soothe her, and in doing so admitted that he had thought a check would not do.

"I did bring fifty thousand in bills with me. It is in a package that I left in the Park Avenue Hotel. I can destroy this, and get the package in ten minutes."

"And bring a horde of officers down on me?"

"No; you can accompany me, or that young man who brought me here can."

"That young man was myself, you fool."

"Then go with me yourself."

The Brown Robin thought a moment, and finally said:

"I will."

She called for her hat and coat, which was brought by a servant, and to that servant she handed the confession, to retain until she returned.

She led the way out of the house in an energetic way, and, when they reached the hotel, entered the office with the broker.

"Now get it," she said, stopping within twenty feet of the desk. "No tricks. I shall watch, and my punishment will be swift, no matter what occurs to me."

Mr. Mountain went off and passed into the private office behind the counter or desk, and for a brief second was lost to sight to the Brown Robin, as he passed behind a high safe.

But she saw him go with the clerk to the safe and receive a package, and return with it to her.

Without a word she led the way out of the hotel and back to the house they had just left.

Entering the parlor again, Mr. Mountain tore off the wrapper to show the bills within, and held it out to her.

She called for the confession, and, receiving it from the servant, held it out to Mr. Mountain, who took it as she took the package of bills.

Mr. Mountain assured himself it was the original by a hasty glance. The Brown Robin was tearing the wrapper from the package.

When she opened it and shifted the bills she fairly screamed.

The package was a dummy, only one bill being on the top.

She sprang forward, but she faced two revolvers leveled at her.

"You are my prisoner, Brown Robin. I am not Mr. Mountain, but Chick Carter, the detective. Mr. Mountain stayed at the hotel that he went to with you. I came in his place."

The woman stepped on the button she had boasted of, and bells sounded in the house.

At the same instant Chick gave a shrill whistle.

A door crashed in and the plate glass of a front window was broken by the heavy blows of a hammer.

Patsy sprang through the window, with revolvers up, and Nick Carter through the door, followed by Mr. Mountain.

Nick met two men dashing down the stairs, the first one of whom he struck in the face with the butt of his revolver, knocking him senseless, and grappled with the other.

Patsy had sprung at the servant woman, who had shown fight, to find she was a man in woman's clothes, and he found his hands full.

Chick had easy work in overcoming the Brown Robin.

It was a fight soon over, however. The two men Nick had attacked in the hall, finding the door open, fled through it.

The other man, in woman's clothes, was overcome by Patsy, and, with Nick's aid, bound.

Though beaten, the Brown Robin was game.

"Well, Mr. Carter," she said, "I have come to the end. I was told you would overreach me if I met you. You have. I did not think you would. I thought myself smarter than you."

"You were very easy," said Nick, quietly. "I could have taken you yesterday, when I dined with you, in the Lexington Avenue house, as Mr. Cary."

"You?" she cried. "You did that?"

"Oh, yes, Mrs. Clymer. You do not offer your cheek to me today."

He imitated perfectly Mr. Cary's voice.

This was too much for the Brown Robin. She seemed to feel worse over this deception than over her arrest and defeat. Nick saw that she had been wounded in her conceit. Finally she said:

"Well, if I am no better than that, I deserve to fail. Lock me up."

The Brown Robin and her servant were taken to the station house and locked up.

"Your imitation of me," said Mr. Mountain to Chick, "was so good that when I passed behind that safe and saw you there waiting for me I was startled, though I expected to find you there. It was capitally done. I congratulate you."

"Congratulate the chief, Mr. Mountain. It was his play from start to finish, and he made me up."

The compromising photographs of Mr. Cary, together with the plate, were easily recovered in the house in which they were taken.

Nick's inquiries into the life of the Brown Robin showed that she had been engaged in a criminal career almost from the moment that she had eloped with the man Stymers from Mr. Mountain's employ, though at one time she had been on the stage and at another time a newspaper writer.

Stymers was a bank burglar, who had led her into crime. Her criminal career had been most successful, and the first check called in it was when she met Nick Carter and his faithful band.

She received a long sentence, and it is hardly likely that she will ever again embark on a career of wickedness.

CHAPTER XI.

AT THE DOG SHOW.

Next day was "blue Monday" with Nick, and he decided to try the Dog Show at Madison Square Garden as a cure for the "dumps."

After luncheon he set out to visit the Garden, little dreaming what fresh adventures were in store for him as the result of that visit.

He had barely entered the hall than a prominent banker, known for the keen interest he took in the development of the dog, and who was one of the officers of the society under whose auspices the dog show was held, greeted him with the remark:

"Of all men, Mr. Carter, you are the man I most wish to see. Some miscreant is poisoning our dogs here. The fourth animal is just now dying from a dose—all valuable animals."

"Have you suspicions?" asked Nick, scenting mystery at once, and nothing loath to tackle another puzzle now that he had placed the Brown Robin behind prison bars.

"Not the slightest suspicions," replied the banker, "although the owner is making wild charges and threats, but, then, that is from her grief."

"Her?" asked Nick, in surprise.

"Yes; Mrs. Constant—poor Al Constant's widow."

"Were all the dogs poisoned owned by her?"

"All of them."

"Do you think it possible that rivalry or jealousy could be at the bottom of it?"

"In the contest here for prizes, do you mean?"

"Yes."

"I cannot believe it."

Nick asked no more questions, and looked over the room.

"Come with me and look at the dog," said the banker.

Nick nodded, and the banker led the detective to a rear room, where he saw a noble setter dog writhing in agony on a blanket on the floor.

A well-known veterinary surgeon was laboring over the dog, and a beautiful woman of thirty, regardless of her costly raiment, was kneeling at the dog's head, soothing and petting him, the tears streaming from her eyes, while she murmured:

"My old Don! My poor old Don!"

The dog's eyes were glazed, and Nick saw at a glance as he came up that the dog was dying.

But from time to time, the poor beast would turn a look of deep affection on the beautiful woman and lick the hand that soothed and petted him.

"Mrs. Constant." said the banker, "here is Mr. Carter, the celebrated detective. I have hopes that I can persuade him to look into this case."

"It is too late to save my poor old Don," said Mrs. Constant, looking up. "As for the miscreant, I know him. He is——"

"One moment," hastily interrupted the banker. "What you have to say as to charges and suspicions say to Mr. Carter alone. He is to be trusted, and his advice will be well worth following."

Mrs. Constant looked up at Nick, smiling through her tears, and said:

"Very well. When can I talk to you, Mr. Carter?"

Handing her his card, Nick said:

"Come to my house when you can."

"I will do so," said Mrs. Constant, "as soon as I have seen poor old Don cared for and my other dogs out of harm's way."

Now the dog had another spasm, and it proved to be his last. He stiffened out and died.

Nick turned away and went into the show room to inquire as to the manner in which the dogs on exhibition were guarded and cared for, and in doing so passed half an hour inspecting the dogs.

At the end of that time, as he approached the center division, he saw Mrs. Constant standing beside a dog with her hand upon its head.

He lifted his hat in salutation, and was surprised to see her state of wonder and doubtful return of the recognition.

He smiled as he thought swift forgetfulness of himself was not flattering. Excusing it on the ground that she was troubled over the death of her favorites, he passed on into the street and went home, where he related the peculiar occurrence that had successfully driven away his fit of the "blues."

A short time after his arrival the servant announced Mrs. Constant.

Nick directed that the lady should be shown into the room he was occupying.

Edith, Nick Carter's wife, who was also in the room, arose to go, but before she could leave the apartment, Mrs. Constant entered, and exclaimed:

"Why, Edith!"

Edith responded by running across the room to Mrs. Constant, crying:

"Why, Blanche!"

All this was very surprising to Nick, who could not imagine how it was that his wife knew his client.

But, as he listened, he found that before Edith's marriage Mrs. Constant had been a member of the same theatrical company with Edith, and, like Edith, had left the stage when she married.

Then that which had before puzzled him was made plain.

He knew that he had seen Mrs. Constant before when presented to her by the banker at the dog show. It was all explained. He had seen her on the stage as Blanche Romney.

When at length the ladies had finished their renewal of old times, Mrs. Constant turned to that which had brought her to Nick.

"I hardly know how to begin my story, Mr. Carter," she said, "but I will tell you how I came to be an exhibitor of dogs at the show. My late husband was much interested in developing a certain strain of setters.

"As I am a great lover of dogs, I took a vast interest in the kennel, and soon came to know quite as much about it as he, taking my part in the management and supervision of it.

"I came to know what he was striving to do, and so, when he died and left all his dogs to me, I determined to carry out his plans and continue the kennel.

"Mr. Constant died very suddenly. The doctors called it apoplexy. He was in good health and was stricken down without warning.

"It is too late now to determine it, but I cannot rid myself of the idea that foul play was at the bottom of his death."

"When did he die?" asked Nick.

"Nearly two years ago."

"At his home?"

"He was brought home, but was taken ill at his club. I had gone over to Philadelphia early in the morning, not to return until the next day, so he dined at his club. The doctors insisted that he had been imprudent at the table, eating and drinking too much.

"Mr. Constant was a free liver, and that gave a basis for their decision. But if I tell you that Mr. Constant was a wine-drinker, do not believe that he used it in excess. He did not.

"Now I come to that which is unpleasant. His marriage to me was not agreeable to his family. They opposed it bitterly.

"I did not know that until after marriage. Whether it would have changed my course if I had, I don't know. His family is very aristocratic, and I was a poor girl, of humble origin, working for wages on the stage.

"We were happy in our life together, but our marriage separated him from his family. He was independent in having a small competence, and a share in the income of a large estate, held in trust, his for life and to be his children's after him, if he had them, which, by the way, he had not.

"I was telegraphed for, and reached him in time to have him die in my arms, but he never recognized me.

"When he was dead I found that he had left his own small fortune to me, but his share in the income of the estate did not become mine.

"I have been advised that I have a right to it, but to get it would mean a lawsuit, and I am comfortable and in plenty without it.

"Now, then; at the time of my marriage there was a man, Eric Masson, moving in the same club and social circle with my husband, who, while pretending to be on friendly terms with him, was his bitter enemy.

"He wanted to marry me. From the first I had disliked him. It was not indifference to him; it was positive dislike for him on my part.

"I had rejected him before I met Mr. Constant. When he learned that Mr. Constant was attentive to me, and that I was likely to marry, Masson warned me not to do it, saying it would be well for neither Albert nor myself.

"He circulated stories as to myself, which had much to do with my husband's family's opposition, and one of them reaching my husband's ears, who was then my *fiancée*, resulted in a violent quarrel between the two, ending in Albert giving Masson a thrashing.

"Though the differences were afterward healed, I know that he worked to my husband's injury always.

"Masson was one of the party with whom my husband dined on his last day.

"My husband had not been dead two months when he renewed his attentions to me, declaring that he had been waiting for Albert's death to step into his shoes.

"I drove him away from me angrily, telling him that I loved the memory of my husband too well to insult it by taking Masson as his successor.

"Since then he has been my vindictive enemy, making trouble for me when and where he could, starting scandals as to myself.

"He tried to take my kennel of dogs from me, declaring that Albert had sold them to him on the day of his death.

"He began a suit at law to obtain the dogs, going so far as to intrigue to get me to hire some creatures of his about the kennel, so that they might steal the dogs for him.

"In short, I have been persecuted by him ever since my husband's death. He is the only enemy in life that I have, and I know he is at the bottom of the poisoning of my dogs."

"I suppose," said Nick, "that this Eric Masson is the broker of that name—the yachtsman?"

"The same person," replied Mrs. Constant.

"Are you prepared to tell me the nature of his persecutions of you?"

"Yes; at any time."

"I do not want them now," said Nick, as Mrs. Constant showed signs of attempting to recite them. "Now, as to the injuries he attempted to do your husband. Can you prove those charges?"

"Yes; after my husband's death I found among his private papers a package, which tells it all. My husband must have gathered them for a purpose that his death defeated."

"Can you let me have that package?"

"Yes; whenever you like."

"Will you let me have it at once?"

"I will bring it to you tonight."

"Very well, Mrs. Constant. Say nothing to anybody that you have given the case to me."

"Masson will know it."

"Why?"

"If he does not know now, he will in a short time, that I have come to see you. He has me under espionage—every step I take he has followed."

"So bad as that?" asked Nick.

With this Mrs. Constant went away, after saying to Edith, who had been an interested listener, that now, having met again, they must not lose sight of each other.

"What do you think of it, Nick?" asked Edith.

"A rather strange story, but there is more behind it than she has told—perhaps more than she really knows. When you knew her what sort of reputation did she bear?"

"The very best," declared Edith. "Blanche was a good girl, Nick. She was so light-hearted and full of spirits in those days, so gay, that sometimes she was misunderstood, but there was not the least harm in her."

"Well, Edith, I fancy you will have some detective work to do."

"In what way?"

"She knows more than she thinks she does. You must get her to talk confidentially to you, and these things may crop out.

"Again, there are things she shied away from telling me, especially when you were present, but she will tell them to you."

"I'll do what I can."

After dinner that evening Nick went out for a short time, and, returning, as he was about entering his house a carriage drove up and some one, leaning from it, called him by name.

Turning back, he saw Mrs. Constant. He went to the carriage door, and the lady thrust out a package to him, saying:

"I am so glad to have seen you here. I am so hurried—so little time. It's the package—Blanche, that is, Mrs. Constant, you know. By-bye, I must hurry. Please tell the driver to go on."

Nick did so, wondering at her haste, and as the carriage drove off entered his house.

CHAPTER XII.

DEAD IN HER CARRIAGE.

Nick sat down to study the package Mrs. Constant had given him, having some knowledge of the persons the package was supposed to tell about.

He knew Albert Constant had been a man of no occupation in life, living on his income; that his family was wealthy, and about the most exclusive in the city.

That his marriage to Blanche had been violently opposed by it, not alone because she was an actress, but because she was of that rank of life which his family believed was much below his own.

He also knew that Albert Constant had quarreled with his family because of this marriage, and as a consequence had withdrawn from society.

Of Eric Masson he knew less. That he moved in the same social circle as that in which the Constants were leaders he did know, and that he was not a popular member of it.

He also knew that he was a broker in Wall Street, and, if there were not charges of sharp practice against him, there were mutterings of them, while it was whispered that at poker with his friends he won too steadily and too heavily.

There were scandals also rumored about as to his private life, all of which, however, had not as yet affected his standing in the social world.

The papers of the package were not easy of understanding, nor did they tell a complete story.

Among them were letters from Masson to Albert Constant and copies of replies from Constant to the same. But the package was principally made up of memoranda in the handwriting of Constant, which was disjointed and seemed to be mere guides for the memory of Constant to be used at some future time.

It all indicated, however, as Mrs. Constant had said, that at some prior time Masson had done Constant an injury, and that, though Masson denied it, Constant was gathering the proof of that injury.

Nick spent the evening over the package, and at bed-time laid it away with a dissatisfied feeling that it did not confirm the charges Mrs. Constant had made.

The next morning, on coming down to the breakfast table, he found Edith sitting horror-stricken over the newspaper.

In answer to his anxious inquiry, his wife extended to him the newspaper, pointing to an article, the mere glance at which informed him that Mrs. Constant had been killed in her carriage the night previous.

Reading the account attentively, Nick found that it was a murder, but by whom it was not even suggested.

Beyond the fact that when the driver arrived at the destination he had been given, he discovered that the person he had driven was dead within the carriage, and that the surgeon, on being called, had quickly discovered that death was the result of a bullet from a small revolver entering the brain immediately back of the left ear. None of the circumstances were given.

Comparing the time, Nick concluded that the murder must have been committed between thirty minutes and an hour after she had driven up to his door to give him the package of papers over which he had spent the time just prior to going to his bed the night before.

The account was not informing, and was but little more than mere announcement of the discovery of the murder, except that it told who the dead woman was and who her husband had been.

Edith was much distressed over the fact that death should have come in such shocking form to her friend, and so shortly after her old associations had been renewed.

Nick devoted some time to soothing and calming Edith, and then sat down to his breakfast, determining that as soon as it was over he would begin an investigation.

But before his breakfast was over he received another shock, though of a different kind.

A note was brought him, evidently written that morning, from Mrs. Albert Constant, asking him to call upon her at once to consult with her on the new horror that had come into her life.

He was astounded. He picked up the paper again to read the article telling of Mrs. Albert Constant's murder. There was no mistake. He had read aright.

It was distinctly stated that the murdered woman was the widow of the late Mr. Albert Constant, and even the poisoning of her dogs at the dog show was talked of. And yet he held in his hand, written that morning, a letter from the woman the paper said had been murdered in her carriage the night before.

"It is incomprehensible, Edith," he said. "There can be no doubt about this letter, and it speaks of a new horror."

"Perhaps," said Edith, "she was not killed, but only wounded."

"The newspaper account particularly says that the ball entered the brain behind the ear," said Nick. "Any one receiving such a wound as that could not write a letter within twelve hours, if she ever could. No; it is not to be accounted for on that ground. I fear this letter was written prior to her murder, for early delivery this morning, on the discovery of some new happening like that of the poisoning of her dogs."

He arose from the breakfast table, saying:

"I shall go to her home at once and try to reconcile what now seems to be a mystery."

He went out of the house at once, and to the residence of Mrs. Constant, which was in the lower part of West End Avenue.

Arriving, there were unmistakable evidences of a tragedy within the house.

In front of it, on the pavement, were a number of people gazing with idle curiosity at the front of the house.

Drawn up at the curbing was the undertaker's wagon, sure testimony that some one within the house was dead.

As Nick mounted the steps, the door opened and the coroner came forth.

"Ah, Mr. Carter," said that official, "you are expected. I have done all that I can do here at present. I presume you will begin an investigation. I hope that you will.

"At present it is a dense mystery. I cannot give you a single point. All that we know is that the woman was killed somewhere between nine and half-past nine last night; that she was shot in the back of the head, and that death followed immediately. But who shot her we have no more idea after working all night than we had in the beginning."

"What are the circumstances?" asked Nick.

"Very meager," promptly responded the coroner. "The lady came from a dressmaker's establishment, and before entering her carriage told her driver to drive directly home to this place.

"As soon as he heard the door close, he drove off, making but one stop on his way here, and that at Fifty-eighth Street, where his carriage was blocked for a minute or two.

"Arriving here, as the lady did not get out, he got down from his box and opened the door, to find her unconscious. He gave the alarm; the woman was carried into her home, and a doctor soon coming pronounced her dead."

"No one was known to have been in the carriage with her?" asked Nick.

"No. That is the great mystery. I was disposed at first to look upon it as suicide. I have not abandoned that idea entirely yet, though all the physicians and surgeons who have examined the body say it is not probable.

"However, the body lies in the parlor. Go and look at it, and after you have made your first investigation, I shall be obliged if you will come and talk with me about it."

The coroner stepped back and opened the door for Nick to pass through, closing the door after him and going his way.

Nick passed into the parlor, and there found Mrs. Constant lying in the box the undertaker had provided.

He stood looking down upon her face, thinking that death had brought its changes and sharpened peculiarities of features that he had not noticed in life.

While he looked, the undertaker came from a rear room, looking at him inquiringly. Nick said, quietly:

"I am Mr. Carter, the detective."

"Oh, yes; Mrs. Constant is expecting you. Indeed, she is very anxious to see you."

Nick looked up in great surprise, saying:

"Mrs. Constant?"

He pointed to the body lying within the box.

The undertaker smiled in a melancholy way, and said:

"That is what has puzzled and confused people so. But let me take you to Mrs. Constant. She has been asking every minute if you have come."

Nick followed the undertaker up the stairs to the door of a room in the front of the house, at which the undertaker rapped lightly.

A maidservant opened the door, and when the undertaker said that Mr. Carter was there, flung it wide open, saying:

"Come, Mr. Carter, Mrs. Constant will be glad to see you."

As Nick stepped into the room, the maidservant spoke to a lady sitting in the corner, telling her that Mr. Carter was there.

The lady arose immediately, and advanced to meet Nick.

At once Nick saw that she was Mrs. Constant in the life. Her face showed the distress she was suffering, for it was pale and haggard, and its lines deeply marked.

The resemblance between the woman before him and the one lying still in death in the room below was astonishing.

Mrs. Constant took Nick's hand, attempting to speak, but broke into uncontrollable sobs.

However, she controlled herself in a few minutes, and said:

"This is the end, Mr. Carter. It is the last. It can go no further."

"I cannot understand it," said Nick. "The paper said it was you who was killed."

"I wish it was myself who had been killed," cried Mrs. Constant. "It was my twin sister, Ethel. But it was I he intended to kill."

The word twin sister explained everything that had bewildered him, as in a flash.

"I did not know that you had a twin sister," said Nick.

"Yes, I had," said Mrs. Constant, sadly. "She came to live with me a week ago. She was so happy to come, and this is the end. She died for me."

"Prior to her coming to live with you," asked Nick, "where did she live?"

"In Philadelphia."

"Had she spent much time in New York with you?"

"Not much time," replied Mrs. Constant. "Only for short visits at long intervals."

"Did she have many acquaintances in this city?"

Mrs. Constant, as in a flash, saw the end toward which Nick's questions were tending, and said, hurriedly and impatiently:

"Waste no time on that, Mr. Carter. Ethel had no acquaintances in New York, except a very few that she had made within the past week. She was killed because the one who killed her thought it was I who was in the carriage."

"I know that you think so," said Nick. "But I was trying to explore the possibility of the other view."

"It is wasted time, Mr. Carter. Ethel knew no one in New York, nor had relations with any one who would do such a thing."

"Could any one have followed her from Philadelphia?"

"No," said Mrs. Constant, earnestly. "Ethel was a good girl; she had no secrets apart from me, and no man had entered into her life in any way. She lived a very quiet life at home, and if there had been any love affair of hers or any one persecuting her, I should have known it. My secrets were hers and hers were mine."

"It was not you, then," asked Nick, "who came to me with that package last night?"

"No. I was detained at home by a caller, and as Ethel was going over to a dressmaker's in Sixth Avenue, I asked her to take that package to you first."

"What time did she leave here to go?"

"It must have been nearly eight o'clock. We were going out last evening, but the dress Ethel was to wear had not been sent home as promised, and Ethel wanted to go for it."

"When she gave me that package," said Nick, "she said she was much hurried. But all the time I thought it was you."

"Yes, the resemblance between us was so great that all our lives we have been mistaken for each other, even by intimate friends. This resemblance is the cause of the announcement in the papers this morning that it was I who had been killed."

"There was no one in the carriage with her when I saw her," said Nick.

"And no one when the carriage arrived home," replied Mrs. Constant. "But a man did get into that carriage, supposing I was in it, and killed her. I know who it was, and so do you."

Nick raised his hand, warningly, and said:

"Mention no names, Mrs. Constant. Charge no one with so awful a deed. Trust to me. I will investigate that line to the end, but let your suspicions be unsaid, or, if you must talk of them, talk only to me."

Mrs. Constant first turned impatiently away, but as impulsively turned back and placed her hand in Nick's, saying:

"You are Edith's husband as well. I will trust everything to you."

"That is good," said Nick. "Now a practical question. The driver of that coach, who was he?"

"The same as my own coachman. I have an arrangement with a livery stable near by, by which I have the same carriage, horses and driver by the month. The carriage is used by no one but me, and the coachman drives nobody but me."

Securing the address of this livery stable and the name of the driver, Nick hurried to the stable, telling Mrs. Constant that he would return soon.

He found the driver without difficulty, and from him learned the course taken by Ethel Romney and the places she had called at.

The story he told was a straight one.

He had been summoned shortly before eight o'clock, and had turned out so quickly that he was at the Constant residence a few minutes before eight o'clock.

He had first driven Miss Romney to the dressmaker's, in Sixth Avenue, where she had got out. She was gone but a few minutes, and, coming out, said that she would have to return to that place. Then she had instructed him to drive to Mr. Carter's house, where she had seen Mr. Carter without getting out of the coach.

After that she had driven back again to the dressmaker's, where she remained possibly twenty minutes, and, coming from there, she had seemed quite vexed.

She told him to drive directly home, and he had followed Sixth Avenue, intending to go up by way of Fifty-ninth Street.

She had made no stop on the way thither, and the carriage had not stopped except for a minute or two at Fifty-eighth Street, where the way had been blocked.

Arriving in front of the Constant residence, as she made no effort to get out, he had got down to see what the matter was.

Then he thought she had fainted, and, making an outcry, people had come from the house. They had carried her in, and he had driven off to the stable.

The man, whose name was Rawson, was positive that no man talked to Miss Romney, except Nick himself, during the ride. He was positive that no one had entered the coach with Miss Romney at any time.

"Are you certain," asked Nick, "that while you were standing in front of the dressmaker's the second time that some one did not enter the coach?"

The man replied that he had seen no one attempt to.

"But it is possible, isn't it," asked Nick, "that a man might have got in there and you not know it?"

"It might be, sir," said Rawson, "but it isn't likely."

Nick turned away. The man had evidently given all the information he had.

He went back to Mrs. Constant, with no light shed on the mystery.

CHAPTER XIII.

POSSIBILITIES.

Nick had summoned his faithful aids, Chick, Ida, and Patsy, to meet him at his apartments on his arrival. He found them awaiting him when he got home, and, without waste of time, sat down to tell them the incidents of the new case they were engaged on.

"Of course," he said, in conclusion, "you will see that in the occurrence of this murder, the poisoning of the dogs slips away into minor importance.

"Yet, if Mrs. Constant's suspicions are correct, the same person is responsible for both.

"In that way, or that view of it, it becomes important to trace out that poisoning."

"The thing stands this way, then," said Chick. "If Mrs. Constant is right about the murder of her sister, she is right about the dogs; if she is wrong about the dogs, she is wrong about the murder."

"As usual, Chick," said Nick, "you state the whole thing in a nutshell. So, as the dog business is more easily followed than anything else, we will get into that investigation first."

"Don't treat Mrs. Constant's suspicions too lightly," said Ida. "I think you will find that she has kept back her strongest reasons for suspecting Masson. She has wanted you to guess them. Edith, as her friend, could get them from her."

Nick looked up at Ida, sharply, and said:

"That is very shrewd, Ida."

Turning to Patsy, he went on:

"I want you to take up the dog end of this case, Patsy."

"I am aching for that," replied Patsy. "I'd rather run down a man who would kill a dog like that than anything else. But I say, chief, put me next to that swell banker. He's one of my kind."

Chick and Ida laughed at this, and Nick said:

"You shall have a note to him. As for you, Ida, you must go to Philadelphia.

"There is this possibility, that the murder of Ethel Romney came out of her life in that city, before she came to New York—some trouble that she had there.

"You must look into that, and we must know all about the life, habits, and even the romances, if any there are, of Ethel Romney. Here is a list of people who would be likely to know about her."

He handed her a slip of paper he had prepared for her, and went on:

"There are other possibilities that we must look into. There is that of suicide.

"It is possible, but not probable.

"Unless the girl had something back in her life, Ethel was more likely to look to the future with pleasure than otherwise.

"She had come to live in plenty and elegance with a sister to whom she was much attached.

"Then, there is the possibility that the murder was the outcome of an attempt by some fellow, bolder than usual, who managed to get into the carriage, supposing that the woman in it had money or jewelry with her.

"All these possibilities must be examined and run down before I am willing to take up the suspicions of Mrs. Constant as to Masson. But that does not mean that we shall not keep Masson in view.

"These things will be undertaken by Chick and I."

Nick now went to the desk, and, writing a letter, handed it to Patsy, saying:

"You want to get to work at once, Patsy, while the trail is warm."

Patsy hurried away, and Ida, saying that, unless the chief had further instructions, she would go, too, followed the lad out of the apartment.

"Now, Chick," said Nick. "To send Edith to Mrs. Constant, and then you and I will take up the most difficult part of the work."

In a few moments these two shrewd detectives were on their way to the neighborhood of the Constant residence. As they were riding uptown in the car, Nick said:

"Mrs. Constant's theory is that Ethel was killed by a person who had intended to kill her, but was misled by the strong resemblance between Ethel and herself.

"That resemblance is great," admitted Nick. "I was misled by it myself twice—once shortly after I had been introduced to Mrs. Constant, and again when Ethel brought that package to me from Blanche Constant."

"But, chief," said Chick, "you did not know at that time that Mrs. Constant had a twin sister; the mistake was a natural one. But if Masson was as well acquainted with Mrs. Constant as he seems to be it would be strange if he did not know of that twin sister."

"And would not have been easily misled," said Nick. "You have struck a point that must be investigated."

"And there is a point on the other side," said Chick. "The hard thing in adopting the theory of Mrs. Constant is that a man of the kind Masson is should commit murder, especially in cold blood.

"Now, suppose that Masson did not know of the twin sister, suppose he climbed into that coach under the notion that Mrs. Constant was in it. Since it was Ethel Romney, she, of course, denied that she was Blanche or that she knew Masson, perhaps, to his anger, leading to the murder and the reason for it."

"That is," said Nick, "supposing it to have been Masson, and that he lost his temper, he lost control of himself, in that denial."

"Yes, that is what I mean," said Chick.

"Well," said Nick, "it all means that we have plenty of work to do and a lot of vexatious little inquiries. Whoever it was that got into that coach, whether it was Masson or some one else, in my opinion crept into the coach while it was standing in front of that dressmaker's establishment to which Ethel Romney went."

This conversation had occupied the greater portion of their trip uptown.

As they stepped off the car, Nick saw the man Rawson, who was the driver for Mrs. Constant. He appeared to be looking for some one.

Rawson brightened up as Nick approached, and said:

"I have been looking for you, Mr. Carter, because I have got something to say. I have been thinking over that ride last night, and especially since you asked me today about its being likely that any one got into that carriage."

"Yes, have you thought of anything more?" said Nick.

"Well, yes," said Rawson. "It isn't much, but, then, I ought to tell you. You see, I didn't think much when you asked me that question, but since I have.

"The lady was in a great hurry to get back home, and as soon as she got into the carriage from that dressmaker's I touched up the horses and started off at a good gait.

"I didn't think much then of it, but I am thinking now that as the lady got into the coach I heard a sort of cry or scream from her, but the door slammed shut right after it, and I was off at once."

Nick looked at Chick, and the latter said:

"It looks, chief, as if you were right as to when the person got into the coach."

"Yes," said Nick; "that would look as if the man was already in the coach, and the noise that Ethel made was a cry of surprise at finding some one there."

Turning to Rawson, he said:

"It looks like a very important point, Rawson, and I wish you would keep up thinking about it. Any little thing about the whole matter tell me of."

What answer Rawson might have made to this was prevented by a man who was evidently a stableman, coming up and addressing Rawson, not knowing who the two were the coachman was talking to. He said:

"I say, Rawson, it's true, isn't it, that you drove the woman that was killed in the coach yesterday?"

"Yes, it's true; worse luck," said Rawson.

"Well, say," said the man, "the papers say there wasn't any man with the woman in that coach. I say there was. What do you say?"

"I say there wasn't," said Rawson.

"Well, you're wrong there."

Rawson was about to deny this somewhat strongly, but Nick stopped him, and said to the man:

"What do you know about it?"

"I know there was a man ridin' with her."

"How do you know it?" asked Nick.

"Why," said the man, "I was standin' in Sixth Avenue talkin' with a friend when I saw my friend here, Rawson, pulled up in front of a swell dressmaker's.

"Then I see his lady, the one he drives for, get out and go into the dressmaker's.

"Well, 'twan't any of my biz, and I wasn't lookin' sharp. By and by I happened to look at the coach, and there was a swell in it."

"Are you sure of that?" asked Chick.

"Sure. But, anyhow, my friend breaks away and I gets on the trolley to go to the stable. When I gets up to Fifty-eighth Street I goes into a saloon.

"When I had put away a couple of beers, I comes out and I stands in front lookin' at a block a big truck loaded with iron had made, when I see Rawson pulled up.

"Then I see my swell guy in the coach open the door on the other side, get out, shut the door after him, and slip over to the other side."

"What's your name?" sharply asked Nick.

"What's that to you?" replied the other.

"Johnny," said Rawson, "this is Mr. Carter, the celebrated detective."

The man started, a little frightened, and immediately became far more respectful.

"My name is Johnny Moran," he said.

"What is your business, Moran?" asked Nick.

"I am a stableman, sometimes drivin' for a livery stable right near where Rawson works."

"He's all right," said Rawson. "We worked together in the same stables before, and he is a good man."

"I have no doubt of that. He looks like it," said Nick. "Now, Moran, what did this man you saw in the coach look like?"

"Well, he was a swell."

"Describe him as near as you can."

The man seemed to be embarrassed, and hung his head, as if trying to think hard.

"I didn't just see his face," he said, at length. "He had on a shiny hat, and whiskers all around his face, that were dark, and the clothes he had on were swell."

"Would you know him again if you were to see him?"

The man shook his head doubtfully, and finally said:

"I don't know about that. You see, I didn't think anything was wrong then, and I wasn't stagging him off for anything. If he was dressed just the same maybe I would, but I wouldn't want to swear to it."

He thought a little while, and then said:

"He was about as tall as him," he pointed to Chick.

Then he went on:

"Seems to me, as he went across the street with his back to me, he had a trick of hitching up his right shoulder."

"How hitching it up?" asked Chick.

"It was more than that—it was a kind of a jerk."

"Is that all you can tell us?" asked Nick.

"It is all that I can think of now."

"If we should want you to go with us some time, where could we find you?" asked Nick.

"You can find me at the stable most any time, and I'll go with you whenever you want me to."

"What you have already told us, Moran," said Nick, "is very important. It has settled one question that we were in great doubt about."

The two detectives turned away, and, as they walked off in the direction of the Constant house, Nick said:

"Chick, luck's with us."

"Nick Carter's luck," Chick said, with a laugh.

"It's luck, whosoever it is," said Nick, "for we might have hunted a long time before we got such direct evidence of the correctness of our theory, that the man entered that coach when it stood in front of the dressmaker's."

"I suppose that we must assume that he did enter there," said Chick, "but we are weak on that evidence."

"We have direct evidence as to how he left the coach after the murder," said Nick. "I think we can safely assume that there is where he did enter the coach. However, there is something for you to do, and that is to go down into that neighborhood and see if you can establish the fact for a certainty that he did enter there."

"Then I had better do it without loss of time," said Chick. "I will go right away."

Thus it was that the detectives separated at that point.

CHAPTER XIV.

A CHANGE OF FRONT.

Patsy had made his way to the Madison Square Garden at once, and presented his letter to the prominent banker.

"I should think," said the banker, as he folded up the letter, after reading it, "that Mr. Carter would devote his energies rather to finding out who killed Mrs. Constant than to finding out who poisoned her dogs."

"Oh, Mrs. Constant is all right," replied Patsy. "She wasn't killed."

"Not killed?" replied the banker. "The papers said so."

"All a mistake," said Patsy. "Mrs. Constant is well, though she ain't happy, for the reason that it was her sister who was killed."

"That beautiful girl!" exclaimed the banker, eager to know all that Patsy could tell him.

Though the lad was anxious to get to work, he was compelled to delay while he satisfied the banker's curiosity.

When he was finally released, which he was with full authority to go to all parts of the huge building, he hurried out into the space where the dogs were benched.

As fond as he was of the animals, however, he paid little attention to them, for he was anxious to make himself acquainted with the attendants.

It was the last day of the show, and the attendance, especially at that hour in the afternoon when Patsy reached the building, was very large.

If thereby movement about the building was made difficult, it was all the better for Patsy, for he was less likely to be recognized.

He spent an hour of close examination without hitting upon anything which could serve as an opening to him.

Finally he engaged in conversation a well-known kennelman of a prominent breeder, leading it to the poisoning of the dogs by degrees.

"Yes," said the kennelman, in answer to Patsy's question, "there was a nasty case of poisoning here. You can bet that it was outside of the bunch."

"What do you mean by that?" asked Patsy.

"I mean it was none of the doggy men that did it, and it wasn't for any show reasons. A breeder, or a man in the business, thinks too much of a dog to do him in that way.

"Setters are not my line. We were only competing in the fox-terriers. So we hadn't especial interest in setters. But I felt as bad over the deaths of those setters as if they had been the dogs I had brought up and cared for.

"It's a mean man that can kill a dog, anyhow—dogs as gentle and sweet-tempered as setters are.

"So I say some one was trying to get square on the lady that owned those dogs, and for reasons away from this show.

"Say, if they ever get down to the truth of it, see if it don't turn out to be a woman that did the business."

This was a new idea to Patsy, and he stood still thinking of it. Suddenly a voice fell on his ear.

"It's him, I'm telling you. Sure. Get out of sight!"

Patsy looked around, without seeing whence came the voice, though two of the attendants were walking off hastily.

Rather from curiosity than from any other reason, Patsy followed them, carefully preventing himself from being seen by them.

When they had reached the end of the aisle, they turned, taking up a position behind a bench, where they thought they were concealed from view.

Patsy crept up as closely as he could, and under the pretense of petting one of the dogs, then listened to their further talk.

"I heard that Nick Carter was onto the case," said the voice Patsy had heard before. "Now his young assistant, Patsy, comes around on the sneak."

"But you ain't sure he's onto the case. Likely he's only come in to have a look at the dogs."

"Look nawthin'! He's here for biz. I am going to get out."

"If you do, you lose your pay. If you drop out now, you get nothing."

"The whack on the other thing is good. Anyhow, I don't want that fellow to get his peepers on me."

"You haven't got the whack, an' I'm ready to bet that we'll get t'rown down yet."

"Go wan," said the other, incredulously.

Patsy cautiously climbed upon the bench and peeped over the division.

Two men in the dress of the hired attendants stood with their backs to him.

As he looked, trying to fix upon some peculiarity by which he could recognize them when in a position to see their faces, a man, who was in his manner and dress of some consequence, approached.

He eyed the two keenly, and the two straightened up as if they expected recognition from the person.

Apparently this person was about to pass by, but he suddenly halted, turned from his path, and went quickly to the bench near where the two were standing, pretending to be much interested in the dogs there.

All of this was seen by the keen-eyed Patsy, and he also saw that as this consequential-appearing person reached the bench, he slipped something deftly into the hands of the two standing ready to receive it.

Not a word was spoken between the three. The passage made, the consequential-appearing man turned from the bench and sauntered on.

Dropping from his perch and keeping his eye on this person, Patsy followed him down, keeping in his own aisle.

As the end was reached, Patsy hurried forward, and, getting close to this person, kept him in sight until he met an acquaintance.

"Who is that person?" asked Patsy, pointing out the man he had been following.

"Don't know," replied the one he accosted. "There's Herrick over there. He knows everybody, and if you want to know badly I'll find out for you."

"Do," said Patsy. "And hurry!"

Patsy's acquaintance hurried off and came back in a moment, saying: "The man's name is Eric Masson."

Though Patsy was rather expecting that reply, yet when he received it, it was with a sort of a shock.

However, firmly fixing in his memory the features of the man Masson by a close inspection of them, he hurried back to the part of the building where he had left the attendants.

They were still in the places where they had stood when Masson came to them and passed to them the mysterious something.

He made a wide circle so that he could come in front of them to observe their faces.

Then he worked up to them gradually, using the passing people skillfully as a screen for himself.

Thus he obtained an excellent view of their faces, and it seemed to him that he recognized one of them, but it was difficult for him to fix it.

He was about to turn away, in an effort to learn who they were, how and under what circumstances they had obtained employment there, when he saw Masson again approaching.

This time he seemed to be stopping for an instant before each of the dogs, but yet steadily edging along to where the two men stood.

Patsy took a chance and moved closer, concealed only by a lady and gentleman, whose next movements might disclose him to the very persons of whom he was trying to keep out of sight.

Finally Masson reached the spot where the two men were standing.

"This dog is not a prize winner," he said, to the one nearest him, who proved to be the one whose features were somewhat familiar to Patsy.

"No; he didn't win anything," replied the man.

Then, in a lower tone of voice, Masson said:

"I want to see you."

"When?" replied the attendant, in the same tone.

"Right away."

"Where?"

"Follow me out and to a place I shall go to."

"Say, boss," replied the other, "if we skip the place now we lose our bones for the four days' hustle."

"Never mind that. I'll make it good. You must get out to me. There's trouble."

"All right," said the other, who had not yet spoken. "If you make good, what you say goes. But it's a ten-case note for each of us."

"All the same. Get off those clothes and get to me."

As the two made a movement as if to go away from the spot, Patsy fell back to a point where he could observe without being seen.

The two went off toward the rear of the hall, and Eric Masson sauntered off toward the main entrance.

There he took a stand as if he was merely watching the passing show.

At once Patsy took in the situation. The men had gone to change their clothes, and Masson was waiting for them to return.

"I must follow them," muttered Patsy. "To do so I must make a change, and I've got to make it quick."

Near where he stood was a door which he thought led into the offices of the kennel club. He dodged through it to find he was correct in his surmise as well as to face the prominent banker.

"What now, Patsy?" asked the banker.

"Only a little makeup," replied Patsy. "I think I'm on to something, and am going to try it."

Much to the interest and amusement of the banker, he drew from his pocket a wig, which he slipped on, and a false mustache, using some color to change his face and eyebrows.

"Oh, for another coat and hat!" cried Patsy, casting longing eyes on those worn by the banker.

"I'll swap with you, Patsy," cried the banker, laughing heartily, as he threw off his coat.

The exchange was quickly made, and as Patsy dashed out, the banker, following, cried out:

"I shan't swap back, Patsy, because as it stands now I got the best of the trade."

Patsy laughed, but made no reply. Hurrying out, he found Masson still in the place where he left him.

He passed close to him, and went into the hallway, standing just within the gate, waiting until Masson appeared.

As this person showed up, Patsy sauntered through the gate and down to the outer doors.

Looking back, he saw the two men, now in their street clothes, following at a respectful distance.

Patsy went out on the sidewalk.

When Masson reached it, he turned toward Twenty-seventh Street and rounded the corner.

Patsy was close behind him. Walking at a brisk gait, which he quickened to pass Masson, he saw that that person was going to Fourth Avenue.

Nearing the corner of Fourth Avenue, Patsy put himself in concealment, quite certain that he had not been observed by Masson or the two men.

And from that point he saw Masson turn up Fourth Avenue, followed by the two men.

Now Patsy trailed in behind them.

The way was up Fourth Avenue, only a few blocks, when Masson turned into a saloon on the corner, making a signal for the two men to follow him.

The young detective passed in close behind the two.

A hasty glance about the room showed him that it was well thronged by customers, something he had hoped for.

It also showed him that a partition formed a small room in the corner on the side on which was the bar.

At the end of the bar, nearest this small room, was a large and rather ornamental icebox. At the end of the box, furthest from the bar, and out of sight of it, was a door leading into the hall by which the upper floors of the house were reached.

This door was open and swung back against the partition, leaving a space behind it.

Masson made his way through the customers to this small room, followed by the two men.

He ordered drinks for them, and when they had been served and paid for, he closed the door, shutting himself up with them.

Patsy slipped behind the hall door. He could hear nothing, however.

By dint of climbing upon the door, resting a foot on the door-knob, he brought his ear on a level with the top of the partition.

The effort paid him.

"There's a lot of trouble," said Masson's voice, quickly recognized by Patsy. "In the first place, Nick Carter has been put on the case."

"That's bad," said one of the others.

"Why bad?" asked Masson.

"Because he's a wizard to get at the bottom of things."

"Well, it isn't likely he'll spend much time on this matter, for he's got something bigger on hand. But that isn't what I am after just now. Listen to me.

"Nick Carter was put on the case. The woman has charged me with being at the bottom of the thing. However, there was a change, and that gives me a chance to do a thing I want to have done.

"Nick Carter won't pay much attention to this thing for a while."

"That's where you're off," interrupted the voice Patsy had first heard. "One of his best men was in the Garden this afternoon. He's there now on the snoop."

"You're wrong, old man," muttered Patsy to himself. "I'm here, on the sneak."

"Who?" asked Masson, anxiously.

"Patsy Murphy," replied the other. "I dropped to him as soon as I saw him."

"Are you sure?" asked Masson.

"You bet he's sure," said the other. "He's been through Patsy's hands, and he knows him."

"That's so," said the first one, "and he left his mark on me so he'd know me again. I sneaked when I saw him."

"Well, if that's so," said Masson, "it makes it all the more necessary that the thing moves as I have planned."

"This woman's sister was killed last night."

"No; the woman herself," said one of the voices.

"Don't contradict me," said Masson. "It was the woman's sister. I've got it straight. That may make some little trouble for me, but not much. It will make more if they get onto the other job.

"But I want you two out of the way to make sure that they don't get on. Take a trip to Chicago, St. Louis, or the devil, for four or five weeks. I'll pay for it.

"Now, then, you see what I mean. Will you get out right away? I'll stake you well."

"I'm game to go on the next train," said one of the two.

"I ain't so ready to go," said the other, "but if it cuts any ice I'll do it."

"Well," said Masson, "it will cut a good deal of ice with me. I can't afford to take any chances now. I wish now that I'd never gone into the job, seeing what turn things have taken.

"But the thing is, are you ready to go?"

"Yes."

"When will you go? Tonight?"

"Yes."

"Where to?"

"Chicago, if you say so."

"Well, I do. It is now near five o'clock. Meet me at half-past seven at the Forty-second Street Station, and I'll hand you the tickets and the stake. Is that settled?"

There was a movement of chairs as if the three men were rising, and Patsy slipped down from his perch and from behind the door.

He was out in the saloon in a position to see them when they came from the room.

"I needn't worry about Masson," said Patsy to himself. "He can be picked up at the station. I'll follow the others to find out who they are."

His chase after these two was not a long one, though it did carry him to the Bowery, to which place the two hurried.

The two toughs, for such, indeed, they were, reaching that famous thoroughfare, quickly made for a saloon which was well known to Patsy through frequent visits to it in the way of business.

So skillfully had his shadow work been done that neither of the two toughs had even seen him.

Entering this place close behind them, Patsy was surprised and not gratified to see within it an old acquaintance, Bally Morris.

But what had rather annoyed him he quickly saw was likely to turn out to his advantage.

No sooner had this Bally Morris seen the two Patsy was following enter, than he went up to them and began a quarrel with them, charging them with having gone back on him in some matter.

It was clear to Patsy that the two had no wish for a quarrel at the time, and he saw them get out of the place as soon as they could.

And he changed his tactics at once. Slipping out, he tore off his beard and false mustache, letting the two go where they would, believing that he would get trace of them at half-past seven at the Grand Central Station.

Having got into his own proper person, he went back into the saloon to find Bally Morris.

That amiable young person recognized Patsy at once, and was not, apparently, anxious to see the young detective.

"Oh, ho," thought Patsy. "He's afraid of me. He's been up to something and thinks I am on."

Asking Morris to take a drink with him, he said:

"Who were the two guys you were wanting to scrap wid, Bally?"

"I don't know who dey is. I hed a muss wid 'em las' night to a rag spiel."

"Oh, come off, Bally. Don't play me dat way. Gimme it straight."

"Honest, I don't."

90 | NICHOLAS CARTER

"Say, Bally, you couldn't be honest if you tried. Well, I ain't on to anythin' you've been doin', but I want to know who dose fellers are, see! If you don't give it, why——"

He stopped, looking Bally in the face, steadily and threateningly.

"Well," at length said the East Side tough, "dey ain't no fr'en's of mine. Dere names is Al Crummie and Bill Graff."

"Crooks?"

"Well, dey ain't straight goods."

"Where is dere hang-out?"

"On de block below. What dey been doin'?"

"Poisoning dogs, I guess."

Bally looked up at Patsy with a laugh, as if he did not believe him.

"Dat's all I know," continued Patsy. "Up to the dog show. Dey was hired there."

"Well," said Bally, "de're mean enough."

Patsy had now gotten all he wanted, and he hurried off to find Nick Carter and to report.

CHAPTER XV.

CLOSER TO MASSON.

Chick was present when Patsy made his report of the afternoon's work, and listened with interest to the remarks Nick made on it.

"Patsy has settled one end of the case in pretty short order," said Nick. "The dogs were poisoned by these two men, Crummie and Graff, who were hired to do it by Masson. What further work there is to be done on that line is only that of making the proof strong. Patsy's work was quickly done, and well done."

"I had a good deal of luck with me," said Patsy, modestly, though much pleased with the praise of his chief.

"Luck, Patsy," said Nick, "usually comes from the right use of your head, and seizing hold of opportunities when they present themselves."

"Well, chief," asked Chick, "how does this triumph of Patsy hitch on to the murder end of the case?"

"There is where the puzzle is," remarked Nick, thoughtfully.

"This morning," said Chick, "we said that if we found that Masson was not responsible for the death of the dogs it would go far toward putting Masson out from under the suspicion of murder. Does it work the other way when we find that he is responsible for the poisoning?"

"I am afraid that is the way we figured this morning," said Nick, with a smile. "But after hearing Patsy's report, I am even more puzzled as to Masson.

"If he was guilty of that murder, he is a cool-blooded wretch to talk of it, as Patsy reports he did."

"Yes," said Chick, "his nerve is great. It seems he knew it was not Blanche, but Ethel Romney that was killed."

"Don't forget, Chick, that at the time he was talking to these men all the world knew. The evening papers by that time had corrected the error of the morning."

"True enough," said Chick, "I had forgotten that. So there is no point in that."

"But, chief," cried Patsy, "what are we to do about the lads that are going to Chicago tonight?"

"Let them go," replied Nick, quietly.

"Let them go?" repeated Chick and Patsy in the same breath.

"Yes; it will be easy enough to get them when we want them. The chief thing is that I want Masson to think that he is right; that we are not paying any attention to the dog end of the case; and, to convince him, if we can, by our action that we have no suspicion as to him as the murderer."

"And then?" asked Chick, who was at a loss to follow his chief, who was laying out a plan so different from his usual course.

"Then I shall have every step he takes shadowed and every move he makes watched."

"And yet you do not believe that Masson killed Ethel Romney?"

"It will not do to say that, Chick. I have told you that I am more puzzled over this case than any I ever had to do with. I will admit to you that, starting with the suspicions of Mrs. Constant, and her reasons, all the indications are just as she suggests—that Ethel Romney was killed by Eric Masson, supposing her to be Blanche Constant. But when it is all done, I cannot make up my mind that he did do it.

"Now, I propose to settle that question beyond dispute."

"Patsy," said Chick, suddenly, "what sort of looking man is Eric Masson?"

"About your height," said Patsy, "brown beard and hair, straight nose, pretty high, eyes close together, so dark as to look black, set well back in his head, dresses very swell."

"Good!" exclaimed Chick. "Now, chief, a man of exactly that description appeared in front of that dressmaker's place in Sixth Avenue, to which Ethel Romney went, just after Ethel was there the first time, and hung around there so long that three people had their attention attracted to him.

"One of them saw the carriage drive up a second time, saw the lady it carried get out a second time, saw this man dart out of an adjoining doorway and follow her as she passed through into the place, speak to her, come out again and get into that carriage.

"This same person saw the lady come out and attempt to enter the carriage, heard a little cry from her as she stepped in, and saw the man hurriedly close the door of the coach.

"There is something for you to crack, chief."

"That is what you picked up this afternoon when you left me?" calmly asked Nick.

"Yes."

"It confirms the stories of both Moran and Rawson. It makes the indications point all the stronger toward Masson.

"Now, I'll give you something stronger than that. Ten minutes after Ethel Romney drove away from home, Eric Masson called at the Constant residence, asking to see Mrs. Constant.

"The servant who opened the door told him the lady had just driven away in her carriage.

"The servant supposed she was telling the truth, for she had mistaken Ethel for Mrs. Constant. In response to the question as to whether Mrs. Constant had gone out for the evening, the servant replied she thought not, as she had heard Mrs. Constant was going to her dressmaker."

"Knowing all this you still have doubts, chief?" asked Chick.

"Patsy," asked Nick, "does Eric Masson walk with a hitch or a jerk to his right shoulder?"

"I saw nothing of it?" replied the lad.

"Chick," said Nick, "Masson was in his club from six o'clock in the evening until ten at night. Three men stand to swear to it."

"What time did Ethel Romney leave her home last night?" asked Chick.

"About eight o'clock."

"It's a puzzle; more puzzling the deeper you get into it," said Chick. "If these three men stand firm, Masson can prove an alibi, if charged."

"Chick, one man stands ready to swear that he saw Eric Masson in Fifty-eighth Street at nine o'clock, for he had just looked at his watch as he saluted Masson.

"Another stands ready to swear that he met and spoke to Eric Masson at about half-past nine, at the corner of Fifty-seventh Street and Fifth Avenue."

"And this is the result of your inquiries since I parted with you?" asked Chick.

"You think that instead of clearing things they are worse muddled."

"It would look that way."

"Well, you're right. I can't even imagine an explanation of these contradictions."

Further conversation on this line was interrupted by the coming of Mrs. Carter, who had been spending the afternoon with Blanche Constant.

She was quite excited, saying:

"It has been a distressing afternoon. Blanche's grief is almost robbing her of her senses. She blames herself so much that she did not guard Ethel against the dangers she was exposed to."

Turning suddenly to her husband, she said:

"Nick, how is it that you can doubt for a moment that Masson is the man that murdered Ethel, thinking she was Blanche?"

Chick was about to speak, but Nick checked him, saying:

"Edith, you know, I usually want proof before I believe a man guilty." Continuing, he said:

"When, having been rejected, Masson learns that Blanche Romney was about to marry Albert Constant, he tells her it will be well neither for herself nor for Constant if she does. It was not nice or manly, yet there is nothing in that to justify a belief in murder."

"But——"

"Blanche thinks he injured her husband. That is only suspicion. She hints at foul play in Constant's death, but it is based only on the fact that Masson dined at the same table. At the very best, it is only suspicion.

"She thinks that Masson killed her dogs, but she has no proof. It is only suspicion."

Patsy looked up in great surprise at Nick when he said the last words. Then he saw that Nick had a purpose in the way he was replying to Edith.

"Well, it is not suspicion when he entices Blanche into an empty house, where he is alone, is it?" cried Edith, quite heatedly.

"What is that you are saying?" asked Nick.

"I didn't mean to speak of it," said Edith, "for Blanche is so afraid of the scandal of it. But the grass was hardly green over the grave of her husband when Masson renewed his attentions to Blanche. That was bad enough in itself.

"She drove him away angrily, and yet he persisted in writing to her until she returned his letters unopened.

"Then one day, having by some means learned that Blanche was be-friending a poor family, he enticed her to go to see that poor family at a certain house.

"When she entered the house the poor family was not there, but Masson was, and he was alone.

"Then he told her that she was compromised by entering that house, for every one in the neighborhood knew that a bachelor lived there, and had seen her enter.

"Blanche only got out of the house by drawing her revolver and fighting her way out.

"One day, when Blanche was giving a reception, for which she had issued cards, five or six most notorious women entered, having received cards, to scandalize her, and one acknowledged that she had been hired by Masson to go there.

"Then, when Blanche sent for him and threatened him with arrest and prosecution if he continued the persecutions, he declared that he would continue them until she married him; that if she wanted to live it could only be as his wife——"

"Now," said Nick, springing to his feet, "we have something substantial to go upon. I knew there was something back of all this indefinite suspicion of Mrs. Constant.

"It required Edith's sympathy to get it out.

"What an infernal scoundrel the fellow is!

"What is true," he continued, "is that we have for the first time knowledge of a threat on the part of Masson to kill Mrs. Constant.

"That becomes serious. Now we have a new motive for work.

"Patsy, you must be at the Grand Central Station to see your friends, Crummie and Graff, off to Chicago. Let them go, thinking that nobody suspects them.

"Then take up Masson's shadow. That is to be your work for the present.

"In the meantime, I am growing alarmed about Ida. She was to wire me before this from Philadelphia."

"Don't worry, chief," said Chick. "Ida knows how to take care of herself. If she has not wired you, it is because she means to turn up from that city this evening."

"I hope so," said Nick, uneasily.

Then the four went to dinner.

CHAPTER XVI.

IDA IN TROUBLE.

When Patsy set out to be present at the departure for Chicago of his two new acquaintances, Crummie and Graff, Nick and Chick accompanied him to the station, in order that they might become familiar with the appearance of Masson.

Under Edith's recital of the tale told her by Blanche Constant of Masson's persecutions, the latter person had assumed a new importance in Nick's eye.

Arriving at the station, Patsy quickly espied the two East Side toughs.

They were roaming about the large room, evidently looking for some one, and not finding him.

"It begins to look," said Patsy, "as if Masson had thrown 'em down."

"Yet," said Nick, "when you heard him talking to them, he seemed to be most anxious to have them get out of town, didn't he?"

"Yes," replied Patsy. "It was his idea. He proposed it to them."

"There may have been a new turn in the game," said Nick.

He had hardly said this when a man stepped out from a group of persons and walked over to the two, speaking to them.

Surprise was plainly shown on the faces of the two toughs when they were addressed, but the expression quickly changed to one of recognition.

This man was about the height of Chick, but he was smooth-shaven.

The three detectives, moving up more closely, saw this smooth-shaven stranger hand a small envelope to one of the two. Then he took from his pocket two small packages, handing one to each.

Patsy, who had edged away, so that he could get a clear view of the stranger's face, came back to Nick, saying:

"Great Scott! The fellow has given himself a clean shave."

"Shaved off his whiskers and mustache?" asked Nick.

"Sure," said Patsy.

Nick made no reply, but Chick said:

"If the fellow looked no better before than he does after shaving, I pity him."

"He looks a lot worse," said Patsy.

Chick laughed, and Nick remarked:

"He is a foolish man."

The doors leading to the train shed were now thrown open, and the gatemen began to call the train.

The two toughs shook hands with Masson and passed through the gate, on their way to the train they were to take.

Masson turned to go to the exit to the street, and in doing so passed close to the three detectives, apparently without recognizing them. If he did, he made no sign of it.

He had gone but a few steps beyond this little group of detectives when he encountered a party of travelers, consisting of two ladies and two gentlemen. To this party he lifted his hat.

All of the four looked with some surprise upon him, and then one of the gentlemen broke into a laugh, saying:

"Why, you have made an astonishing change in your appearance, Masson."

"Yes," replied Masson, fully at ease. "And not for the better, I imagine."

To this remark no one made reply, but the other gentleman said, lightly:

"It was a reckless thing to do—making such a complete change."

"It was forced on me," said Masson. "A fellow that looks like me has been going about town representing himself to be me, and causing me a good deal of trouble. The only way in which I could stop him was to destroy the resemblance."

"Perhaps he will shave, too," said one of the ladies.

"But he will not restore the resemblance," replied Masson. "It was the whiskers that did the trick."

Their conversation was changed with this, and Nick said to his companion:

"Was that said by Masson for our benefit, think you?"

"It sounded like a throw off," said Chick.

The three detectives passed out of the building, and stood on the sidewalk in front of the main doors, waiting for Masson to make his appearance.

"You must follow Masson when he shows up, Patsy," said Nick.

Patsy moved away, to be prepared for this duty, and Chick said:

"If Masson's words were not intended for us, then they were important in showing that there is another man on the carpet who might be confused with him."

"And," added Nick, "it would afford an explanation of the contradictions that now bother us."

At this moment Masson came through the door and walked briskly up Forty-second Street, Patsy following.

Nick made a signal to Chick, and started after.

Thus Masson was followed to Fifth Avenue, when he turned to the south, going down that avenue, to all appearance unconscious that he was followed.

At Thirty-seventh Street Nick stopped, Chick halting with him.

"I have followed as far as I want," said Nick. "I wanted to see whether he walked with a hitch or jerk of his shoulders."

"Did you notice it?" asked Chick.

"No," said Nick. "I noticed nothing in the man's habits of movement that indicated it."

The two now turned to the west, leaving Patsy to continue his shadow of Masson alone.

This shadow led to a club some distance down Fifth Avenue, in front of which stood two men, one of whom respectfully saluted Masson as he came up.

Masson walked directly to the man, and said, abruptly:

"There will be nothing doing, Denton, until tomorrow night. Then I want steam up and everything ready for a three or four weeks' cruise. I want the launch to be at the old pier as early as eight o'clock, although I may not be there to meet it until ten.

"Now, Denton, I want no mistakes. The same men manning the launch that we have had before. I want the crew off the deck when I go aboard. You alone are to have the watch from nine to twelve.

"I shall be here at the club until midnight. After that I shall be at home until tomorrow. You can reach me any time tomorrow here at the club if you have need to."

Masson was about to go into the clubhouse, and the two men to whom he was talking had moved off a short distance, when a third man came running up, saying:

"There is a mistake, Mr. Masson. The funeral does not take place tomorrow, but the day after."

"Are you sure," asked Masson.

"Sure. I got it from the undertaker in charge."

Masson hurriedly called the two men back, and said to them:

"Wait! There may be a change of orders."

Turning to the third man who had come up, he asked:

"What are the arrangements?"

"The funeral is at eleven, and the burial will be at Greenwood as soon thereafter as it can take place."

"Hum!" exclaimed Masson, thoughtfully. "Day after tomorrow then. That changes all arrangements."

He walked off to the two men who had come back and were patiently waiting for him to speak. To them he said:

"The orders I gave you are all off. Come to me tomorrow here for further orders. In the meantime, you can continue preparations for a long cruise. That's all for the present."

The two men went away, and Masson, taking the other by the arm, led him into the house.

Patsy had overheard the whole of this conversation by slipping out into the middle of the street, behind the four persons and climbing into a cab standing empty before the door.

When all had disappeared, he crawled out again and crossed to the other side of the street.

"Now, what does all that mean?" said Patsy to himself. "The first two men were from his yacht. That's clear. And Masson is going on a long cruise. That's clear, too. But who was the other man, and what's that about a funeral?"

He stood thinking a little while, and then suddenly exclaimed:

"Gee! what if it's the funeral of that Miss Romney? Well, I'll shadow him for a while if he comes out, for Masson's going to stay in the club."

Shortly after the man who had entered with Masson came out, and leisurely walked off into the direction of Broadway, closely followed by Patsy. It soon became apparent that he had no particular business on hand, nor any special place to go to, but was lounging from saloon to saloon.

"It's eating up time for nothing following this chap," said Patsy, to himself. "I'll give him the drop, and start after the chief to find him."

Acting upon this thought, Patsy hurried to his chief's residence, to find that Nick had just come in with Chick.

He reported the conversation between Masson and the three men that he had overheard, to the great interest of the two elder detectives.

When he was through, Nick said:

"Masson has shipped off to Chicago the two men who were his instruments in the dog poisoning affair. Now he is going away for a long cruise himself."

"But, chief," said Chick, eagerly; "how about that funeral? His going away seems to be tied up with that."

"I was coming to that," said Nick, "and it is the most important thing. The undertaker, having been given full charge, had appointed tomorrow as the day of the funeral, but Mrs. Constant, having learned this, postponed the funeral another day, on the ground that it seemed like hurrying Ethel into the tomb to have the funeral so soon.

"Now compare this fact with what Patsy overheard between Masson and that third man who came up, and we can conclude that the funeral Masson is interested in is that of Ethel Romney.

"It appears, then, that Masson is determined to begin his cruise on the day of that funeral. Why?"

"It is very strange," said Chick, "and I take it we will have to find that out. It can't be, chief, that it is to be explained on the simple ground that Masson wishes to attend that funeral?"

"Dismiss that idea, Chick," said Nick. "Masson will not attend in any event. No, we must look deeper than that for an explanation."

The three were silent a moment, each busy with his own thoughts, when Nick said:

"This calls for action. We may be forced to show our hands before we are quite ready."

"We can hardly let Masson go out of sight," said Chick.

"And yet," said Nick, "we have not enough basis on which to detain him. We have got to meet this another way.

"The name of his yacht is the *Derelict*. When he is not aboard, it lies in the East River, off Twenty-third Street. Patsy, there is some work for you to do."

The famous detective got up from his chair, and began pacing up and down the apartment, keeping it up for a long time. When he stopped he dropped again into his chair, and said:

"I am satisfied that this move of Masson's bears some relation to the case we have in hand. What, I am not able to figure out. But we must get 'onto' it, to use Patsy's words, and Patsy, you must be the one to get 'onto' it."

"All right, chief," said Patsy. "But you must tell me how."

"Didn't you tell me once that some summers ago you were on a yacht as a steward for a little while?"

"Yes."

"Well, I think you will have to try and hire out as a steward on the *Derelict*."

Patsy laughed, and replied:

"Or as an able seaman?"

"Any way, so long as you get aboard," said Nick. "That's the most important thing we have to do at present. And you haven't much time to do it in, either."

"And it isn't an easy thing to do," said Patsy; "but I'll start the ball rolling tonight."

The little clock on the mantel of the room struck the hour of ten, and Chick said:

"If you are going to start the ball tonight, you'll have to start it very soon, for it's ten o'clock now."

At that moment the servant entered the room with a telegram, which she handed to Chick.

Tearing off the envelope and opening the folded paper within, Chick read aloud:

"'Am in trouble.'"

Chick hastily glanced at the top of the dispatch, and exclaimed:

"Philadelphia! The deuce! It's from Ida."

"How do you know?" asked Patsy. "Is it signed by her?"

"There's no signature," said Chick. "But I know it's from her."

Nick was already on his feet, and he said:

"And she wants help or she never would have sent the message. Chick, you and I start for Philadelphia now. We have just got time to catch the next train that leaves for that city."

"Do I go, too?" asked Patsy.

"No," said Nick. "We leave you in charge of the case. Get on to that yacht if you can. I fancy that that's where the work must be done. We can't tell how long Chick and I will be away. But, if anything important turns up, wire me to the old place in Philadelphia.

"Now, Chick, we must be off."

Nick and Chick hurried away, and Patsy went off to start his own difficult work.

CHAPTER XVII.

A NEW SIDE.

Ida met with an experience unusual to her on her trip to Philadelphia.

While riding on the cars she perceived that a man and woman, fellow-passengers, were eying her with no little curiosity.

What had attracted their attention she was at a loss to know, and for a time it irritated her.

But, turning to the window, she, by interesting herself in a magazine, tried to forget it.

And, becoming interested in her story, she did forget it, and was only started from her interest by seeing a man seat himself in the chair next to her.

For a time she paid no attention to this person, except to observe that he was a man apparently of thirty-five, wearing a closely-clipped brown beard and brown mustache, his hair cut very short.

Her book slipping from her lap gave this man the opportunity for which evidently he had been looking.

Picking it up, he returned it to Ida, receiving her thanks for his courtesy, and then attempted to enter into conversation with her.

However, making no reply to his remarks, when he persisted she swung her chair about so that she presented her back to the man.

She was aware that the man was angry, but she gave little heed to that, merely turning to satisfy herself that the man was not the one who, with the lady, had a little time before annoyed her by their close watchfulness of her.

She had not sat in this position but a little time, when the lady before mentioned arose from her seat, and crossing the car, sat down in the empty seat which Ida was now facing.

"Pardon me," said the lady; "I take this seat and speak to you for two reasons. One is rather a kindly one, and the other wholly selfish and curious.

"I perceive that you are being annoyed by the man on the other side of you. I saw that by sitting beside you and talking with you I could put an end to his annoyances."

This the lady said in a low tone that could not be heard by the man at the back of Ida.

When Ida had thanked her for the interference the lady went on, but now in a much louder voice.

"My selfish and curious reason is one not so helpful, but I hope you won't think it impertinent.

"My husband has recognized you as the celebrated Ida, the aid of the famous Nick Carter, of whose exploits I have frequently read.

"I have long admired you, wondering how a woman could do such brave things as I have known you to do. So I wanted to know and talk with you."

Though much annoyed at thus having her identity revealed in a public place, Ida could not refrain from meeting the lady pleasantly, for in the lady's speech and manner there was, after all, much that was complimentary.

Yet it was an uncommon experience for Ida. She knew that Nick, Chick and Patsy were subject to such happenings, and were often compelled to resort to disguises to prevent accidental recognitions.

She did not care to be so conspicuous as recognition made her, but a moment's thought told her that, after all, no great harm was done, since her mission to Philadelphia could hardly be called a secret one; that is, secrecy was not required in doing her work.

But, what gave her the most annoyance was that she was conscious that the man on the other side of her had heard the lady, had started into unusual interest, showing a little agitation and had swung his chair around so as to bring his ears nearer to the two.

However, he soon got up, going to the other end of the car.

After this the lady and Ida chatted pleasantly until the train drew into the great station in Philadelphia, when the lady rejoined her husband, and Ida left the car.

The first thing that Ida did on reaching the street was at once to set out for the house in which the family of Blanche Constant and Ethel Romney lived.

As she passed the City Hall she saw, standing on the lower step of the main entrance, looking at her intently, the man who had attempted to get her into conversation on the cars.

Making no sign, and thinking that it was an accident, Ida hurried along, keeping a sharp lookout behind her. It seemed to her that the man was following her at a distance.

And when she reached the street, where she was to take the street car, she thought that she saw the man concealing himself in a neighboring doorway.

Of this she could not be certain, but, when mounting the car, which was a good deal crowded, she had the uncomfortable feeling that the man was on the same car.

"All this may be accidental," said Ida to herself, "but I don't think it is."

Arriving at her destination she left the car hastily, and, reaching the curbstone, turned to watch the people descending from it.

The man who had seemed to follow her was not among those who got off at the corner, but, as she watched the car roll up the street, a man dropped off about midway of the block above, and Ida thought it was the man in question.

This man hurriedly walked up the block in the same direction the car was going, and disappeared around the same corner.

Ida now looked at her memoranda, and found that the house occupied by the family of the murdered girl was in the street on the corner of which she was standing. It was not her intention to visit this house, but she had intended to inspect it from the outside.

It was clear that the houses of that neighborhood were not occupied by the wealthier residents of Philadelphia, but it was also clear that it was a thrifty neighborhood, and that the people living there were at least in comfortable circumstances.

Most of the people whose names Nick had put down on the list he had given her lived thereabouts.

One, however, was a detective friend of Nick's, who, Nick said, would give Ida such assistance as she might need were she to require it.

Ida, however, had determined that she would not call upon this detective unless she were compelled to, by failing to secure what she was after in applying to the other people.

Having observed the house, Ida passed on, intending to call on a woman living on the block below, whose name had been given her by Nick.

As she reached the next corner, to her surprise, as well as to the surprise of the other, she came face to face with the man who had annoyed her previously, and who had just turned the corner.

In his surprise and embarrassment the man lifted his hat and went on.

Ida continued her way, a good deal troubled by the encounter.

Her call on the lady in question resulted in a success that she could not have hoped for.

In fact, she secured information which was complete, and was only confirmed, not added to, by those whom she subsequently visited.

And in this information were revelations of which Nick had not dreamed.

From this woman, who was familiar with the history of the family, Ida learned that Blanche and Ethel were twin daughters of an old actor and actress; that the father had died when the girls were about twelve years of age, and that the mother, after continuing on the stage for some two years thereafter, had married again and left the stage.

The man she had married was a superior mechanic, who had invested his savings in the purchase of a saloon, which quickly became a sporting haunt; he was a widower, with a son aged about eighteen years at the time of his father's marriage.

When his father engaged in the liquor business he had taken the son into the store, who, under the influences, grew to be rather sporty in his tastes and practices.

As the two girls developed they did not get along well with their stepfather, and Blanche, the more spirited of the two, left her home when eighteen to become an actress.

Ethel, however, who had neither a taste nor an aptitude for the stage, remained at home, enduring an unpleasant life.

After Blanche had made what was considered to be a wealthy marriage, the conditions at the Romney home were utterly changed.

George Macrane, the stepbrother, under the suggestion of Donald, his father, became a suitor for the hand of Ethel.

There seemed to be an idea on the part of the father and son that a good deal of money must come from Blanche to Ethel, and that the husband of Ethel must benefit by it.

Ethel, from the first, had resisted these efforts, and was compelled to fight the battle almost alone.

Her mother was evidently a weak woman, completely under the rule of her husband, and joined her husband and his son in their effort to force upon the girl the unwelcome suit.

The girl Ethel had shown more spirit in this resistance than she had displayed in all her life before. It became persecution, for her life was made miserable during the four years that it lasted.

All sorts of annoyances were put upon her. She was not permitted to go out, or to receive company, and, if she talked with any one, especially a man, a great row was made with her.

As the time went on these persecutions were increased.

Finally the girl Ethel, in her distress, had carried her troubles to the lady talking to Ida.

This lady had advised Ethel to tell all her troubles to her sister Blanche, something which Ethel had not done, because of the urgency of her mother not to trouble Blanche with the family affairs.

At length the matter had become so bad that Ethel had permitted Blanche to know how unpleasant was her life at home, with the result that Blanche had insisted that Ethel should come to live with her.

The decision to do so had been met by a terrible row at home, and was only accomplished by Blanche coming over to Philadelphia and actually carrying Ethel off in spite of the opposition of the stepfather and son, which became so much of a quarrel that the elder Macrane, losing his temper, attempted to strike Blanche, and was only prevented by the interference of the mother and son.

Blanche had carried Ethel off, but not until both father and son had threatened that it would not end with that.

Further inquiry on the part of Ida showed that the elder Macrane was a man of almost ungovernable passion, while the son was in much better control of himself, but was sullen, determined and vindictive.

Ida left this lady intending to confirm this story by further inquiries, and, indeed, did so in parts by three subsequent calls.

She said to herself, that at the present rate of progress she was making, she would be able to return so as to arrive in New York by midnight at least.

It was now just growing dark when she set out for the next name on the list.

CHAPTER XVIII.

IN DURANCE VILE.

Ida was led a little distance from the neighborhood in her next call, and to a part of the city that differed in appearance from that in which, up to this hour, she had spent her time.

It was more sparsely settled, the houses further apart and the buildings larger.

As she reached the address of the person she was next to call on, she was met by a rather rough-looking young man, who asked her who she was looking for.

Ida did not like the looks of the fellow, and, as she answered, her hand stole to her pocket where her trusty revolver, which had served her well in the past, safely lay.

Having given the name of the person she wanted, the young tough told her to enter the hall door, climb the stairs and knock at the first door she came to.

She entered the hall as directed, but found it wholly dark.

Stopping a moment to strike a match, so as to see her way, the first faint glimmering of the light showed her the forms of three men crouching at the foot of the stairs.

Instantly the match was knocked from her hand, and, in the intense darkness that followed, she found herself seized both from before and behind.

Though she struggled, she was powerless in the grasps of the scoundrels.

Then something was pulled over her head which seemed like a bag. Naturally much frightened, nevertheless Ida did not lose her wits, and keenly noted every move of the rascals who had seized her, carefully watching for some sign of the brown-bearded man, whom she immediately suspected of being at the bottom of the attack on her.

She was now lifted from her feet and carried farther into the hall. Then she was certain she was borne into the open air. Then again into a narrow passage, up some stairs and into a room, where she was placed on a chair.

The men left her alone, but she could hear them close and bolt the door behind them.

All was as silent as the grave. Outside, from the distance, she could hear dimly the roll of wheels and the noise of the trollies, but that was all.

She tried to tear off the covering that had been put on her head, and found she had no difficulty in drawing it off.

There was no light in the room save that which entered through the windows from the street.

It was little, but sufficient to see that the room she was in was barely furnished. There was a table and two chairs. That was all.

She went to a window and saw that it looked out on the street, but could see no one there.

She examined her pockets and her dress. There had been no attempt to take anything from her. Her revolver still rested safely in her pocket. She felt more secure when she found this had been left to her.

She also drew from her pocket what she had forgotten she had—a blank form for a telegram and the stump of a pencil. Her pocketbook was secure also.

Hearing a noise without the window she went to it again to see that a young lad was crawling along the coping.

Trying to throw up the sash, she found it was nailed fast. Winding her handkerchief about her hand, so that it would not be cut, she broke a pane of glass and thrust her head through it.

The boy was startled and seemed as if he were going to crawl back.

"Who are you?" asked Ida.

"Did they lock youse up there?" asked the boy.

"Yes; how did you know?"

"I was on the stairs and seed 'em."

A thought occurred to Ida. She asked:

"Will you do something for me?"

"If I kin."

Ida took out her pocketbook, and, handing a bill to the lad, said:

"Here's a dollar. I want you to take a telegram for me. It will cost a quarter. The rest of the money shall be yours. Will you take the paper to the telegraph office?"

"Sure. Where's de paper?"

"I'll write it."

Ida hurried to the table and filled in the address of Chick, at Nick Carter's, in New York. Then she wrote these words: "Am in trouble."

She had only gotten so far when she heard quick steps in the hall without, approaching her door.

Without waiting further she rushed to the window and thrust the telegram she had written out of the window to the boy, who snatched it and crawled away in a hurry.

Ida went back to the table, her hand on her revolver.

The bolts were withdrawn and a man entered the room.

At a glance Ida saw that he was disguised, and not skillfully at that.

He crossed the room to where she was standing, the table between them, and stood looking at her intently a moment or two.

Ida returned his gaze. Neither spoke for a while. Then the man said:

"You are Nick Carter's Ida. What is your business here?"

"I have none," said Ida. "I was brought here against my will."

"I mean in Philadelphia."

"That is my business."

"Answer me, or it will be worse for you. You are here on the Ethel Romney case."

"Suppose I am, what then?" asked Ida, boldly.

"Well, you won't do much locked up here, will you?" asked the man.

"Oh, I don't know," replied Ida. "You can't tell."

The man did not know what to make of that answer and did not reply for a moment or two. Then he said, roughly:

"Nick Carter thinks that the one who did the girl came here."

Ida made no reply, but she was thinking hard.

"He's wrong. It was a New York swell. You're working on the wrong lay."

Still Ida made no reply.

"Who does Nick Carter think did it?"

Ida continued her silence.

"What have you got onto since you've been here?"

Ida did not answer that question.

"Why don't you answer?" said the man, roughly. "I'll make you answer mighty quick."

Still Ida did not speak.

The man, losing his temper, attempted to reach her by passing around the table, but Ida edged away until their positions were reversed, and she stood where the man had, and the man was where she had stood.

The door was open behind her. She made a dash for it. The man seemed prepared for that, for he violently pushed the table aside and sprang after her.

Ida, drawing her revolver, whirled about, and, leveling her gun, called out:

"Don't come. I'll shoot!"

The man laughed, sneeringly, and advanced.

Ida fired. The ball carried high, knocking off his hat. But it halted the scoundrel.

Ida sprang through the door, dashed along the hall, finding the head of the stairs and rushed down them.

The man followed, shouting at the top of his voice, apparently calling the name of some one.

Descending the stairs Ida found an open door and rushed through it to see that she was in a small yard.

Hastily glancing about she saw a door in the fence. She sprang to this and found it unlocked. In a moment she was in the street.

But she was hardly through the gate than the man was upon her.

Ida drew her revolver again, but this time, as she leveled it, it was knocked from her hand by a man who had come from behind a tree.

She was overpowered again. In the struggle she tore the disguise from the man who had followed, and the hasty glimpse she had satisfied her that he was the man who had accosted her on the cars—the brown-bearded man.

This time they tied a handkerchief over her eyes.

"She's the devil's own," said the voice which Ida thought was the voice of the one from whom she had just escaped.

"You say she belongs to Nick Carter?" said another voice. "So she is."

"She won't get away this time," replied the other.

The two attempted to pick her up again.

While her eyes were being bandaged, Ida had seemed to make no resistance, but was busy in taking something from her pocket.

But when the two lifted her up, she wriggled out of their grasp, sinking to the pavement, where she tried to do something with her hand.

The two pounced on her again, and this time lifted her clear from her feet, and not gently, either.

It did not appear that they carried her again through the gate by which she had escaped, but up the street a short distance and into another hallway.

But she struggled with every step, throwing out her right arm and bringing it into contact with everything she could strike.

She did this so regularly that it seemed as if she had a purpose in it, though what it was, was by no means clear.

She was carried up a pair of stairs and put in a room again, and, as before, seated in a chair.

"There," said a voice that she recognized as that of the brown-bearded man, "I reckon you'll stay here for a while."

Ida lifted her hands, which had been left free, and tore the bandage from her eyes.

She was not in the same room, and it was lighted so well that she could see that she had made no mistake in supposing that one of the men was the one who had traveled from New York at midday with her, and that the other was the tough who had, in accosting her, induced her to enter the dark hallway.

She had not spoken a word.

"She's game," said the tough.

"I should say so," replied the other. "But we'll take some of the gameness out of her before we get through with her."

The two withdrew, locking and bolting the doors behind them, leaving Ida alone in the dark to think over her strange plight, and whether her telegram would reach Chick, and, if it did, if Chick would find her.

CHAPTER XIX.

A DASHING RESCUE.

It was after midnight before Nick and Chick reached the streets of Philadelphia.

Before they drew into the station, Nick had said:

"We'll waste no time, but go directly to the neighborhood in which Ida was to do her work."

"If it's not in the main streets, the people will have been asleep these two hours," said Chick.

"All the same," said Nick, "if Ida is in trouble, as we believe, I don't know the girl if she won't find some way of letting us know where she is, if we get into our neighborhood."

So it was that when they left the station, they followed the route that had been taken by her earlier in the afternoon, getting off the car at exactly the same corner that she had done.

Here Nick stopped a moment, to think of the memorandum he had given Ida as his guide to their further movements.

"Chief," said Chick, "if we are now on the ground where Ida has been working, we ought to be careful how we move around, for fear some one will drop to us."

"You are right about that, Chick," said Nick, leading the way down the street—the same one Ida had gone.

As he got opposite a house, about the middle of the block, he stopped short, and said, in a low tone, to Chick: "That's the house Ethel Romney left to go to New York, where she met her death."

"The old home of Blanche Constant, then?" asked Chick.

"Yes," replied Nick. "I only know it by the fact that this is the street and that is the number."

At that moment there was a noise, as if the door of the house was being opened, made distinct by the silence which reigned in the street.

The two detectives immediately slipped into concealment of the first doorway, and watched.

The man came out, carefully closing the door after him, and, coming down the steps, stopped a moment on the sidewalk, where the light from the arc lamp fell full on his face.

"Brown-bearded and brown-haired," remarked Nick, in a whisper.

The man under watch finally turned and walked off toward the lower corner. Chick slipped out and across the street, directly in his rear. He did not attempt to follow the man, but watched him walk away. Then he slipped back to Nick on his tiptoes, saying, eagerly:

"By thunder, chief, that man walks with a hitch and jerk of his right shoulder."

"I thought I saw that myself," replied Nick. "Under other circumstances we'd follow that man, but now our business is to find Ida."

As a matter of fact, they did follow the man, but only because their ways were the same.

At the corner below they saw this man pass through a door, which Nick and Chick sized up to be the back door of a drinking saloon.

They let him go, and Nick led the way to the house of the woman on whom Ida had first called.

This was not guesswork. He recalled that he had advised Ida to see that woman immediately on arriving in Philadelphia.

It was with some difficulty that the woman was aroused, and when she was, her means of communication with them was through the window of her bedroom. It did not take long for Nick to learn that Ida had called on her, and that she did not know whither Ida had gone on leaving her.

"The first point is made," said Nick to Chick, "for we have found that Ida reached here and began work. Now we will follow her up."

Taking a position under the arc light near by, Nick took from his pocket some papers, and, after examining them, said:

"I fancy we can travel Ida's course pretty straight for a while. Come along."

Thus, without delay, they called at each of the next three places Ida had gone to, and in the order that she had, compelled in each instance to arouse people from their beds to answer their questions.

But at the end of this journey they were, to use the words of Chick, "up against it."

What line Ida had traveled, and to what address she had gone, they had no way of judging.

Although Nick had given her the name of a person to call on, he was unable to tell where that person lived, and had advised Ida that she would have to find out on her arrival in the city. He could only tell that it was in a certain neighborhood, information which he had obtained from Blanche Constant after the murder.

However, assuming that this was her next direction, they went thither in what Chick felt to be a rather hopeless search.

Reaching that part of the town, they traveled the streets in all directions without hitting upon any indications of Ida's tracks.

Coming to one corner, which they had passed several times. Nick said: "Here's a street that we have not been over yet; let's try it."

"I am afraid," said Chick, as he followed his chief down the street indicated, "that we will find other streets that we will travel until daylight."

He had hardly gotten the words out of his mouth than he stopped short and dropped down on his knees, looking at something intently on the pavement.

Nick halted, looking with great interest at what his aid was doing. He saw him take from his pocket a small lantern he always carried with him, and turn the light on a particular spot of the pavement.

"What is it, Chick?" said Nick.

"Red chalk marks," said Chick.

"Signs?" asked Nick.

"Not our signs," said Chick, "though they seem to look as if there had been an attempt to make one. But, chief, I'll bet my life that this is the same chalk we use."

Nick bent down over the spot, and saw that the pavement was made of red brick; that it would have been difficult to have made one of the signs that they used between them, and that in this case the marks only seemed to have been hastily made without any form whatever.

He stood up erect, looking at Chick.

"Could those marks have been made by Ida?" asked Nick.

"I am guessing that they were," said Chick. "Anyhow, I gave Ida a piece of that chalk, and told her she ought to always carry it with her, for she could not know how useful it might become."

"Let's look a little farther," said Nick.

"Wait a minute," said Chick. "If any one comes, play drunk."

Backing up against a tree, Chick suddenly lifted that fine, manly voice his friends knew he had, in a popular song of the day, that rang out on the night air as clear as a bell.

He had sung but a verse, when two men suddenly appeared at the corner beyond them, say a hundred feet away, and Nick began to urge him to come home and not make a holy show of himself in the street, saying that they'd have the cops down on them if he didn't stop it.

He could hear one man say to the other that it was only a couple of drunks, and saw them turn back and go out of sight.

Chick sang another verse, and then both listened.

There was an answer, indistinctly, yet clear enough for them to hear every note. They heard the third verse of the song sung through.

"Ida's here," said Chick.

"Are you sure?" asked Nick.

"Sure!" replied Chick. "I'd know her way of singing in the wilds of Africa."

"Then you have found her," said Nick. "And the next thing is to get to her."

On looking up, he saw nearly opposite where the marks on the pavement were, a door in the fence opposite to where they were standing.

Both he and Chick carefully examined this door and the fence for further marks without finding any.

Then Nick followed up the pavement, until he came opposite the door of the first house to be reached, and there beckoned to Chick, pointing with as much excitement as the great detective ever showed, to long red marks on the brickwork of the door.

"That's the house she is in," said Chick.

Nick tried the door, and found it was locked. It took him but a minute to pick the lock, but this did not open the door, for it was soon apparent that it was barred from within as well as bolted.

Chick was preparing to put his strength against it, when Nick checked him, and said:

"Let's try if there is an entrance from that yard."

Hurrying to the door in the fence and through it, they closed it after them and began an examination of the yard in which they found themselves.

The brick wall of the house, on the door of which were the red marks, made one side of the yard, and at the rear of this side was a door to which they went. This door opened to them on the first trial, and Chick's lantern came into play again to show a hallway with stairs leading up.

They mounted these stairs revolvers in hand, and on reaching the landing, found an open door opposite them.

Turning into this room, the first thing that they saw was a large black cloth bag on the floor, the next a woman's handkerchief, which Chick said belonged to Ida.

It was the handkerchief which Ida had wound around her hand with which to break the pane of glass, through which she had talked to the boy who had helped her.

A hasty examination of the adjoining rooms satisfied the two shrewd detectives that the house was not occupied regularly.

Out into the hall they went again, to follow it to an angle, where it turned sharply to the rear, examining each door that they came to.

Finally, at the extreme end of the hall, they found a door which was not only bolted, but barred as well. Chick went to this door, and tapped on it lightly, but in a peculiar manner.

The signal was so light as to be almost unheard, but it was immediately responded to.

"She's here," said Chick. "Cover me while I take these fastenings off."

In a twinkling the bar was wrenched off and the bolts withdrawn and the door flung open.

Nick and Chick sprang through, with revolvers up and were met with a merry laugh.

"There's no one to fight here but me," said Ida.

She soon satisfied the anxious inquiries of the two that she was unharmed and uninjured in any way, and then Nick said:

"Not another word now until we get Ida out of this place."

"Give me a gun," said Ida. "I lost mine early in the evening."

Chick handed her one, saying that she'd find it a little heavier than the one she was used to having.

"Now," said Nick, "I will lead, Ida follow and Chick behind. Come on."

They passed through the hall and to the stairs, and down them without anybody interfering. But, as they reached the door, it was opened and a man made his appearance.

Ida immediately recognized him, even in the dim light, as the tough who had misdirected her into the dark hallway where she had been seized.

"That is one of them," she said.

The tough, with an oath, called on some one behind him and sprang at Nick.

Possibly if he had known the ready use the famous detective could make of his fists, he would have thought twice over his action.

As it was, he received a blow straight between the eyes which sent him out of the door and on his back to the pavement.

Nick sprang forward through the door at once to meet the second coming up. He did not wait for any action on the part of that fellow, but sent him to keep company with the other, who was endeavoring to get on his feet.

Chick caught Ida and swiftly carried her out of harm's way, through the door and into the street, through which now she had passed for the second time that night.

Nick followed them closely, and in a moment they were out on the corner.

"Take notice of the place, Chick," said Nick. "We may want to come back here again."

The two rascals who had been so severely dealt with by Nick made no attempt to follow them, and it was not long before they were in the street where they could take the cars that would take them to the hotel where they usually stopped when in that city.

It was not until then that Ida told the story of her experience of the night, and of the information she had gained.

After he had listened to it intently, Nick said:

"What you tell us puts an entirely new look upon our case. Chick has picked up a point to add to it, and together they give us some work that will keep us in Philadelphia tomorrow. That brown-bearded man has got to be investigated."

"Yes," said Chick, "and we have got to know where he spent the last three days."

"But what was the meaning of their peculiar treatment of me?" asked Ida.

"They meant to keep you a prisoner," said Nick, "to prevent you from doing work which they had already found was getting too close to them."

Nick got up from his chair, and turning to Chick, said:

"Come, Chick, Ida wants rest after her rough experience, and you and I have got to size up something. Come with me."

CHAPTER XX.

PATSY'S TRIUMPH.

While these events were transpiring in Philadelphia Patsy was endeavoring to set out as a yachtsman.

Chick said that Patsy was like a cat, since he always fell on his feet, no matter how you threw him.

Leaving Nick and Chick starting for their Philadelphia trip, he wandered over to Broadway and from caprice turned into the hotel café where he had left the man who had brought to Masson the news of the change in the arrangements for the funeral of Ethel Romney.

Rather to his surprise than otherwise, he found this man drinking with acquaintances.

Among them was one with whom Patsy was slightly acquainted.

This man knew Patsy had some connection with Nick Carter, but how much he knew Patsy could not tell.

As Patsy was standing near the bar, this man looked up and recognized the lad.

He arose from his seat and crossed to where Patsy was standing, addressing the young detective rather familiarly.

His purpose of rising appeared to be to light his cigar; but he said:

"I want to shake that crowd. They drink too fast for me, and I don't like the gang."

The man who was in relations to Masson called out:

"Are you going, Jensen? Well, don't forget to send me a handy boy for the cabin, as you promised."

"Who is that?" asked Patsy.

"His name is Moore. He is a sort of a hanger-on of Masson, the broker. Don't know what, exactly. But does things for him."

"What does he want of a handy boy?"

"Some one to go as a steward on Masson's yacht."

"I wish you would get me the job."

"You?"

The man called Jensen looked curiously at Patsy for a moment, and then asked:

"Do you mean it?"

"Sure."

"You would take the place?"

"Try me."

"By George! What a go. I'll try it. Ever had any experience that way?"

"I was on the *Gay Flirt* one season."

"Good."

He called Moore aside and whispered to him a while. Moore came to Patsy, saying in an off-hand way:

"My friend backs you for the place. Wages twenty dollars a month and board. Report on board the *Derelict* off Twenty-third Street, at nine tomorrow morning."

He handed Patsy a slip of paper, on which he had written some words, and went back to his companions.

Looking at it, Patsy saw it was an order to the chief steward to put him to work.

Hailing the man Jansen, Patsy prepared to leave, but Jansen followed him out to say:

"I'd give an old button to know your game. But I'll wait to hear the story until I meet you again."

Patsy went off with a laugh, and to bed.

The next morning, promptly at nine, he reported on the *Derelict*, and was promptly set at work.

He was heartily sick of his job before the day was over, for it was hard work he was at, with nothing occurring to relieve the monotony.

About six o'clock in the evening the man he had seen the night before waiting for Masson in front of the club house came aboard.

Patsy soon learned that he was the sailing-master and he had not been on board long before there were orders to pull up and steam down the river.

The yacht was taken around Governor's Island, into Gowanus Bay, and brought to anchor not far from, but out of the track of boats of, the Thirty-ninth Street Ferry.

All things were settled for the night.

The next morning there was much work done in preparation of sailing that afternoon with the owner on board.

Patsy kept a keen eye open for signs of the things Nick expected to occur, for he felt that whatever did occur must happen before the yacht set sail on its cruise.

At twelve o'clock the man who had engaged him as steward the night previous, Moore, appeared on board and entered at once into an earnest talk with the sailing-master.

What the subject of their talk was Patsy was unable to discover, although he made all sorts of efforts to get within earshot.

Whatever it was, was not to the liking of the sailing-master, for he shook his head doubtfully over what Moore was saying. The other was persistent.

Finally, the sailing-master arose, saying in a tone easily heard by Patsy:

"Well, all right, I'll do it. But I tell you, Moore, I don't like it. There will be trouble for some of us, if it keeps up."

"There'll be no more," said Moore. "The Mogul has his mind set on this and——Well, if we don't help in it, some one will be out of a job."

"And some of us take a chance of being in—somewhere else," replied the other, with a bitter laugh.

As he turned away Moore detained him, and there was a further whispered conversation, during which Patsy could see that they frequently looked at him.

Finally the sailing-master called him over and asked:

"Do you know how to obey orders and keep your mouth shut and your eyes closed for an extra wad?"

"For that I do," replied Patsy.

"I size him up as right, Moore," said the sailing-master. "Give him your orders."

He walked away.

"There's something on this afternoon that'll make dollars for you," said Moore.

"All right," said Patsy.

"Well, then," said Moore, "in twenty minutes you'll go ashore and be posted in a certain place, where you can see all around you. And there you'll stand. See?"

Patsy nodded.

"By and by, up on a hill that will be shown you, a man will wave a red cloth. If there are no policemen in sight you will wave a white handkerchief. If there are you'll wave a green one. See?"

"I see, all right."

"Then you'll feet for the launch, and, getting aboard, shut your eyes. See?"

"All right."

"Then you're game for it."

"Game for anything."

Moore went away, but was back again shortly, telling him to follow.

A steam launch lay alongside, into which Moore dropped, telling Patsy to follow.

This launch ran off to a part of the beach rather out of sight and retired.

A broken-down wharf stretched out into the water, and the launch ran up to it.

At a signal Patsy went ashore. Four other men went ashore also, leaving two men aboard, one at the wheel, and the engineer.

Patsy noticed that none of the other men seemed to be of the yacht's crew.

The six picked their way over the wharf or pierway and reached the land.

It was a lonely spot, a large, unbroken waste, few houses or buildings near.

They all followed Moore for some three hundred yards, when he stopped, saying to Patsy:

"This is your post. Now keep your eyes open for policemen. Up on that hill yonder the man will be with the red flag. If the way is clear and nobody down there where we landed, wave this."

He handed Patsy a napkin.

Moore took the other men away. Just then a bell tolled in the distance.

"The devil!" exclaimed Patsy. "We're not far from Greenwood Cemetery."

Then he said again:

"And the funeral is today."

He sat down on a stone and did some thinking.

The result of this was that he took off his coat, turned it inside out and put it on again, looking as if he had another coat on. From his pockets he drew a wig and put that on. He rolled up his cap and put on a slouch hat.

Then he stole up in the direction the others had gone. He passed the man stationed on the hill unrecognized.

Arriving at the avenue where the cars ran, he looked around for Moore. By and by he saw him standing in front of a drinking saloon.

He edged up close to him and saw he was anxiously waiting for some one.

That some one appeared shortly in the person of Masson, from a carriage which was driven up to the place.

"Well?" said Masson.

"It's all right, so far," replied Moore.

"The funeral carriages will be along in a moment."

"Is the driver fixed?" asked Moore.

"Yes; to be knocked off his box, and one of our men to take his place."

"Does she ride alone?"

"No; hang it. There's a woman with her."

Patsy went out and sat on the curbstone. Something—an outrage of some kind—was on foot.

A funeral procession came up—a small one. In the carriage immediately behind the hearse were two women. One he recognized at once.

It was Edith, Nick Carter's wife.

The other was Blanche Constant. He was sure of that from the description he had had of her and a photograph he had seen.

Something of the villainy on foot came to him. He hurried back to his post and again became a steward of the *Derelict*.

His wait was a long one. By and by he saw the red cloth waved by the man on the hill.

He gave the signal of the white cloth—indeed, gave it without care as to whether or not there was any one near or not.

A minute later a carriage came dashing over the hill.

Four men sprang out, one seizing the horses, while one knocked the driver from the box and climbed up himself.

Two others climbed into the coach from either side.

Then the coach made straight for the landing where the launch was.

Patsy started on a run for the little pier, and at the land end waited, well hidden.

As the coach whirled up, he could see within it.

Edith was there, and so was Blanche Constant, but both were unconscious.

Masson and Moore were both there also. The two men—the signal man and the one who had stopped the horses—were left behind.

Masson had planned to seize Blanche Constant as she was returning from the funeral of her sister and carry her off in his yacht.

Edith had been with Blanche, contrary to expectation, and she had been dosed to prevent her from interfering, but was to be sent back to the city.

Patsy's plan was made in an instant—a plan to spoil the plan that had been carefully laid.

He waited until Masson got out of the coach and had lifted Blanche out.

Then he sprang into full view, both revolvers leveled.

"Hold!" he cried. "Put that lady down!"

"What!" shouted Masson. "What the deuce! Moore, look to that fellow!"

The driver made a movement as if to get off his box.

"Jim Grady!" cried Patsy; "if you stir, I'll put a ball into you and pull you in beside for that job of two nights ago!"

"Heavens!" cried the driver, "it's Patsy Murphy!"

He jumped from his box and ran like a deer. Meanwhile Masson was raving like a madman, calling on Moore to shoot the young detective.

Moore did start for Patsy, and with revolver in hand.

Patsy was in no humor for fooling and, as Moore approached, he fired, striking the scoundrel in the shoulder and sending him to the ground with a groan.

Masson, seeing his lieutenant down, dropped Blanche to the ground and rushed like a maniac at Patsy, shouting for help.

The engineer and the wheelman, hearing the shot and the cries of Masson, climbed out of the launch and came rapidly over the rickety wharf.

Patsy saw at a glance that he was likely to be attacked from behind, and, taking deliberate aim, fired at Masson, hitting him in the upper right arm.

Yelling with pain and rage Masson dropped to the ground and Patsy, whirling around, shouted to the two coming over the rickety pier:

"Back, you curs! I'll serve you as I have the others. I'm Patsy Murphy!"

Whether they knew the name, or were satisfied that he would do what he said he would, the fact is that they stopped, and at Patsy's command dropped to the pier.

Dashing up to the carriage, Patsy picked up Mrs. Constant, put her in the coach, and, springing on the box, whipped up the horses.

He was not a minute too soon, for the signal man, the driver and the other one were approaching as fast as they could run.

Indeed, as Patsy drove toward them they made an effort to stop his way, but Patsy, standing up in his box, fired his revolver, right and left, in a way that made them believe that caution was the better part.

So he dashed on toward the avenue.

The shots had attracted attention, of course, and several policemen came.

"I'm Patsy Murphy, of Nick Carter's staff of detectives," cried Patsy. "This is a case of abduction that I have spoiled. The ladies in the coach are Mrs. Constant and Nick Carter's wife. Seize those men of that yacht lying out there."

But, looking out on the water, they could see the yacht was moving out into the harbor under full steam.

Patsy was disappointed, for he would have liked to arrest Masson, but he had saved the women, and that was the important thing.

He first drove them to a drug store, where they were quickly restored to consciousness, and then to the city, having first engaged a driver at a livery stable.

Edith took Blanche home with her, and Patsy was a hero in the eyes of both. But Patsy, getting home, was inconsolable that he had no prisoners.

CHAPTER XXI.

THE MURDERER.

Events developed rapidly in Philadelphia while Patsy was having his fight with Masson and defeating the abduction scheme.

Before they had discussed Ida's information long both Nick and Chick had arrived at the same conclusion.

They believed they had found the murderer in Philadelphia, and that Nick's instinct that Masson was not the person guilty of the murder of Ethel Romney had been right from the first.

"We must move without delay, Chick," said Nick. "Our rescue of Ida will inform this man that we are in town, and he will run."

"To make our conclusions a dead certainty," said Chick, "we ought to prove that George Macrane was in New York on the day of the murder."

"We'll take the chances, and prove it afterward," said Nick, grimly. "Come."

"Where?" asked Chick.

"To see the chief of police."

"At this hour? It is three in the morning."

"He'll have to stand for it."

They went out and woke up the chief of police, who, understanding the situation, summoned two officers, whom he put at the disposal of Nick.

The four then set out for the house of Macrane, arriving there a little after four in the morning.

They approached the house cautiously, concealing themselves where they could watch it.

A light was burning in the third-story window, which Nick fancied was the window of the room occupied by George Macrane.

As they watched, two men came down the street, and, rapping at the door of the Macrane house, asked for George.

They were told that he had not yet returned home.

Chick's sharp eyes recognized one of these men as one of those that had opposed their rescue of Ida.

These two men sat down on the lower step of the Macrane house.

"They mean to wait for George Macrane," said Nick.

They did not wait long, for in ten minutes' time a man was seen approaching from the opposite direction.

The two men stood up to meet him.

What they told him could not be heard by Nick and Chick, but it was followed by a frightful explosion of oaths and curses from George Macrane.

So frantic, indeed, was this outburst, that Nick thought it proceeded from a craven fear of the result.

Touching Chick, and, bidding the officers to follow, Nick slipped across the street, closely approaching the three men before they were seen.

Laying his hand on the shoulder of Macrane, Nick said:

"George Macrane, you are my prisoner. I want you for the murder of Ethel Romney."

The shock was so sudden that Macrane dropped to the pavement in a heap.

If the other two had been disposed to make a resistance they were too much astonished at the charge made against their employer to offer any.

They stared in open astonishment, and made no show of objecting when the officers took them in charge.

George Macrane soon recovered possession of himself, and, rising, said rather tremblingly, to be sure:

"You must be wild to charge me with that. Ethel Romney is in New York."

"She is in Greenwood by this time," said Nick.

"I couldn't have done her—she in New York and me here," said Macrane, growing bolder as he talked. "She's been there a week or more."

"It is useless, Macrane," said Nick. "We know the whole trick. You were in New York yourself. You laid the game up well, but we know it.

"You knew there was a man in New York who was following Ethel's sister; you were told you looked like him; you saw him, and you trimmed your whiskers to be exactly like him."

Nick stopped and looked at Macrane. What he had been saying was purely guesswork, but he saw that he had hit home.

"You called at Mrs. Constant's home at eight o'clock on the night of the murder, giving the name of Masson. You were told that Mrs. Constant had gone out to the dressmaker's.

"You knew that wasn't so—you knew it was Ethel who had gone out, but thereby you found out where she had gone to.

"You went to the dressmaker's and waited till she came. You tried to speak to her as she went in. Then you went into the coach and waited.

"When she came to enter it she saw you and screamed, but you pulled her in and shut the door.

"The coach drove rapidly up the avenue, and during that drive you shot her, for she had told you that she was done with you forever, and meant to live with her sister.

"When the coach was checked, at Fifty-eighth Street, you stepped out, crossed the street, and, going down Fifty-eighth Street, you bowed to a man at nine o'clock, who spoke to you as Masson.

"Half an hour later, on the corner of Fifty-seventh Street and Fifth Avenue, you talked for a few minutes with a man who stopped you and called you Masson.

"You made yourself conspicuous in other places when you thought suspicion could be thrown on Masson.

"Then, when you thought you had done enough you started back to Philadelphia, but one of my aides was on the train. We were on your track. We were bound to land you as we have landed you."

Turning to the officers, Nick said:

"Take us to the lockhouse. Chick, have you hand-cuffs?"

Chick had not, but one of the officers had, and Macrane was ironed.

It was daylight when Nick and Chick returned to their hotel to snatch a brief sleep.

Early in the morning they were out, making the proof strong that Macrane had been in New York.

They wired for Patsy to come on, with Moran and the storekeeper of Sixth Avenue that Chick had dug up, by an early train.

On their arrival they positively identified Macrane as the man seen entering and leaving the coach.

Patsy, on his arrival, reported his experiences with Masson and the rescue of Mrs. Constant and Edith.

Though Patsy told it with all modesty, Nick knew that Patsy had performed a most gallant and heroic deed, and so said, but it was not until he returned to New York that he learned how gallant and brave the deed was.

Speaking of the curious development of the case, Nick said:

"From the first I felt that Mrs. Constant's natural bitterness toward Masson had misled her judgment. I never did believe that he did the murder.

"The strange thing is that Mrs. Constant did not give greater importance to the feeling of Macrane toward Ethel.

"However, she has a hold on Masson now, and if she will follow my advice, Masson will see the inside of a prison for his evil deeds. He deserves it."

But he did not.

When Mrs. Constant learned that she had unjustly charged Masson with the murder of her sister, she seemed to feel that she had done him an injury which she could atone for only by refraining from following up the advantage she possessed.

Masson fled to Europe, so that Mrs. Constant is now free from his persecutions.

Macrane lies under conviction of murder in the first degree, and awaits execution.

He has confessed, saying that he visited New York to force Ethel to return with him, and, finding that he had lost her and all control of her, in a fit of anger he killed her.

Mrs. Constant devotes herself to her kennel, but her grief for the death of her sister is so great that she is a broken woman.

When Patsy wants to be particularly swell, he sports a fine diamond ring that Mrs. Constant gave him in recognition of his bravery when he prevented her abduction by Masson.

The case is referred to by Nick Carter's outfit as "Patsy's Triumph," and as such is not easily forgotten.

www.ingramcontent.com/pod-product-compliance
Lightning Source LLC
Chambersburg PA
CBHW020148180626
46810CB00004B/1782